She

Gadgets cradled Julie in his arms. He took her face, feeling at the base of her neck for the pulse he was sure he wouldn't find.

Suddenly her eyes flickered open.

For a moment they were wide and staring. Then they came to a tight focus on his face.

He bent closer to her. "Julie?" His voice was low and urgent. "Julie, can you hear me?"

The facial muscles around her eyes were the first to move as she tried to speak through the shock. Then her lips moved, and when she spoke, Gadgets was surprised at the clarity of her voice.

"Tell Carl..." she began.

Julie didn't finish the sentence. Her voice simply halted, and her eyes lost focus.

Slowly Gadgets laid her gently on the floor.

Mack Bolan's
ABLE TEAM

#1 Tower of Terror
#2 The Hostaged Island
#3 Texas Showdown
#4 Amazon Slaughter
#5 Cairo Countdown
#6 Warlord of Azatlan
#7 Justice by Fire
#8 Army of Devils
#9 Kill School
#10 Royal Flush
#11 Five Rings of Fire
#12 Deathbites
#13 Scorched Earth
#14 Into the Maze
#15 They Came to Kill
#16 Rain of Doom
#17 Fire and Maneuver
#18 Tech War
#19 Ironman
#20 Shot to Hell
#21 Death Strike
#22 The World War III Game
#23 Fall Back and Kill
#24 Blood Gambit
#25 Hard Kill
#26 The Iron God
#27 Cajun Angel
#28 Miami Crush
#29 Death Ride
#30 Hit and Run
#31 Ghost Train

GHOST TRAIN

Dick Stivers

A GOLD EAGLE BOOK FROM
WORLDWIDE

TORONTO • NEW YORK • LONDON • PARIS
AMSTERDAM • STOCKHOLM • HAMBURG
ATHENS • MILAN • TOKYO • SYDNEY

First edition August 1987

ISBN 0-373-61231-1

Special thanks and acknowledgment to
Chuck Rogers for his contribution to this work.

Copyright © 1987 by Worldwide Library.
Philippine copyright 1987. Australian copyright 1987.

All rights reserved. Except for use in any review, the reproduction or utilization of this work in whole or in part in any form by any electronic, mechanical or other means, now known or hereafter invented, including xerography, photocopying and recording, or in any information storage or retrieval system, is forbidden without the permission of the publisher, Worldwide Library, 225 Duncan Mill Road, Don Mills, Ontario, Canada M3B 3K9.

All the characters in this book have no existence outside the imagination of the author and have no relation whatsoever to anyone bearing the same name or names. They are not even distantly inspired by any individual known or unknown to the author, and all incidents are pure invention.

The Worldwide Library trademark consisting of the words GOLD EAGLE is registered in the United States Patent Office and in the Canada Trade Marks Office. The Gold Eagle design trademark, the Executioner series design trademark, the Able Team design trademark, the globe design trademark, and the Worldwide design trademark, consisting of the word WORLDWIDE in which the letter "O" is represented by a depiction of a globe, are trademarks of Worldwide Library.

Printed in Canada

PROLOGUE

She touched the scar to justify what she was about to do.

Kara took a deep breath. The night air felt cold and clean on her skin and in her lungs. It sharpened her senses and heightened the sense of purpose that she and all the others at the camp felt. She didn't feel like sleeping; instead she thought of what had happened and of what the future held.

It would be soon.

A glittering blanket of stars lay over the emptiness of the desert. The moon had not yet risen above the horizon, although an orange glow behind the hill signaled its approach. The air was so clear and the night so dark that even the faintest stars made streaks of glowing dust.

It made her feel humble, and yet it made her feel chosen.

Kara knew with a quiet certainty that destiny and the forces of the universe had given her a very special thing. It was a legacy that would lead others to freedom; it would liberate the enslaved.

She called it her gift.

Not out loud, of course. She didn't talk about it to any of the others, not even to Mark and Fadi, whom she trusted more than any other people in the world. Kara only called it the "gift" in the special private conversations she had with herself.

But Kara knew that the term "gift" did not begin to adequately describe what had been placed with her. It was like saying a glacier was ice. It did not reflect the magnificence and the magnitude of it.

It was the gift of death.

Kara knew that she was "chosen" in the sense that this gift had been placed with her rather than with someone else. And she knew that although many would be called, only a few would be chosen.

The humility she felt came from the purpose of the gift.

She realized that it was to be used to help others, those who must be freed from the oppressors. In that sense, she was a changer of destiny, a soldier in an eternal struggle, an actor in a play of passion and power.

Deus ex machina.

Kara was proud she remembered that phrase.

She had learned it while attending a private school in France, an expensive and exclusive place to which she was shunted while her wealthy parents traveled the world. The phrase meant an unexpected intervention. She thought it referred to someone who comes out of nowhere and changes the course of history—the cavalry that suddenly appears to save the day just when all seems lost. Deus ex machina, the god that comes from the cosmic machine to alter history.

In her special private dialogues—the secret conversations inside her head—Kara had come to learn that *she* was the god that came out of the machine. She would alter destiny. It was her gift, and it was her duty as well.

The gift of death. The duty of killing.

She must never forget that. She must especially remember it through the pain and the loneliness that were her constant companions.

They had been present when she was a child in that Paris boarding school. They had been there when she was scarred, when she was brutally raped at age seventeen. And she had certainly experienced her share of pain and loneliness during the endless months of training and shooting at the PLO camp some three hundred miles from Beirut that had been her home for the past year. They had been with her for so long that they had become part of her.

Along with the gift came the beautiful sensations she felt when the gift was used.

At first she had felt guilty about the feelings. Something about them reminded her of school, and of being eight years old. But she could never remember the rest of it, although she knew she'd been bad. It was better left forgotten. Best not to think of it, ever.

Best just to accept what was now.

Kara had finally accepted that it was simply part of the grand design that she experience these good feelings when the gift was used. The feelings were not the ultimate purpose of the gift, they served merely to remind her of her duty.

Kara did not doubt that she would do what was expected of her; it felt good to kill. And she was going to get to kill very soon.

She had killed twice already, and after those swift, smooth motions, she had sampled the good feelings.

And soon, within ten days, she would kill again. But this time, it would not be just once. It would be again and again, over and over, all in the struggle against the oppressors.

They had to be stopped.

First Mark and Fadi would strike at the airport. Kara knew they might die in the attempt, but she could not show her concern. Besides, like her, they were the best. They might well survive the attack and live to fight other battles.

And then, after the airport—only a matter of a few days later, in fact—it would be her turn. She would lead the others, and the blood would flow. Her gift would be used, as it was meant to be used.

Many would die at her hand.

The months of training at the desert terrorist camp had hardened Kara's mind and her body until both had become efficient tools of war and insurrection. She had become a highly skilled warrior.

Selection, indoctrination and training. Those were the three mandatory phases that Kara and the other members of her terrorist cell underwent before going on any operation.

The selection had been done initially by persons whose names she had not known. They were shadowy figures, the leaders who had recruited her from her world of protests, coffee shops and off-Broadway plays, from her life as a modern-day beatnik and radical who wrote letters of protest to every major daily newspaper.

Words were okay, they told her. Words were necessary, in fact. Education of the people must occur if the struggle were to be finally successful.

There were many who could supply the words, but there were only a few who could accomplish what she had been selected to do.

Back up the words with action.

Kara had always been an exceptional athlete. Slightly taller than average for a woman at five feet eight, Kara's body was powerfully athletic and feminine. She had the long, graceful legs of a dancer and the broad shoulders of a swimmer. Kara was a highly attractive woman with shiny black hair and an olive complexion.

In addition to her bone structure and size, she had nearly perfect musculature. It was the kind of thing that happened to one in ten million people. The shape and size of her muscles, the tendon inserts, the ratio of bone length, the number of microseconds it took for nerve impulses to react—all had come together in this one, optimum body.

The result was that she possessed the strength and speed that made her physically superior to most human beings, regardless of sex. Kara was the perfect candidate to supply the action to back up the words.

Still, the training had nearly broken her. And strangely, the indoctrination—the constant teachings of revolution and of guerrilla concepts—had been what had helped her survive it.

But even then it hadn't been easy.

First the running. Some of it was long distances, but more of it had been explosive sprints of ten, twenty or thirty yards. Agility drills, dodging and cutting and twisting had been part of the sprints. Then there'd been the jumping, hurdling and running backward.

Kara was put through the climbing and diving and rolling, and the combative arts—striking, parrying, throwing and kicking. And all this before any of the weaponry.

Several of those who had started with her dropped out. It was as if the training were still part of the selection process.

The instructors, men and women alike, seemed to enjoy making it as hard as possible on her. They had singled her out for special attention, attention that was painful and degrading. They always found some fault with her performance, and the penalty was to repeat it. And when the combatives were taught, the instructors had always chosen one person to be the visual aid, the guinea pig, the person on whom the new technique was forcibly demonstrated.

That one person was Kara.

Usually she had to attack the instructor, or place a certain hold or control a simulated weapon so that it appeared she had the advantage. Then the instructor would demonstrate the technique of escape or counterattack.

Inevitably, this meant a painful lesson as the highly skilled instructor broke free and turned the tables.

At first, it appeared that even Kara's marvelous constitution and physique would not be equal to the punishment. Her body weight declined ten pounds, and she began to feel more and more tired as those first few days became weeks, and then a month.

Then, in some mysterious way, she adjusted.

It was as if the various systems inside her became synchronized, and somehow toughened. She had in a sense hit the bottom and then started to rally. Her weight increased, but it was all tight muscle beneath the feminine lines of her body.

And with the physical toughness came a mental toughness.

It went beyond confidence. In fact, it was more of a certainty of herself and her purpose. Added to her physical abilities and concealed by her beauty, the toughness was what completed the project and made her into an almost perfect killing machine.

The last time she was singled out as a guinea pig, it had been Hassim who was giving the demonstration, Hassim, the cruel swarthy pig who took pleasure in inflicting pain during the exercises.

The demonstration had followed the familiar routine.

Hassim told her to apply the neck-lock hold on him, the one he had taught them the preceding week. Now, he would teach them the only way to avoid that neck lock, should it ever be placed on them by an enemy. And after that, he would teach them how to neutralize the avoidance technique, if they were the ones applying the hold. Sometimes it seemed like an endless chain of moves and countermoves, yet all were important.

As always Hassim had sneered his instructions at her.

"Do not hold back," he had said. "This is war, you fat Western piglet, not a schoolgirl's game."

Kara had been aware of the eyes of the others on her. And, as she now thought back on it, she had also been aware that this time it would be different.

"Well, come on," he had commanded. "Try your best to defeat me, Comrade, to keep me in the hold and kill me. I will show how easy it is to escape, especially from the hold of a soft American sow like this one. And then I will show you how easily the escape may be prevented."

Kara had said nothing, but stepped forward to apply the hold.

"Go for it, little girl," he had jeered. "It will hurt you a little now, but it may save your worthless life in the name of our cause later."

She had moved into position behind him and had applied the hold, placing her forearms and wrists just so around his hard, large neck. And she had waited for him to give the signal for the demonstration to begin.

"Now!"

The escape called for him to be moving in one direction, as if lunging, jerking away from her. Then, when she attempted to move with him, and was off balance, he would reverse the motion. As he moved back toward her, he would drive a rock-hard elbow into her solar plexus and twist away.

Hassim had lunged and then reversed the move.

Kara's motion had been simultaneous, and so quick and strong that she was never off balance. When Hassim had attempted the reverse, it was he who became off balance, not Kara. She had not only moved with him, it was as if she were *ahead* of him.

Instead of a potentially crippling—and certainly painful—blow to the pressure point below the inverted V of her sternum, Hassim's elbow strike had been a clumsy push.

Kara had seen it all very clearly, almost in slow motion.

She had turned her body slightly, easily to one side as she had moved. Hassim's elbow had glanced harmlessly off the side of her rib cage. And then Kara had used their combined forces to begin to take him down.

Off balance, he had had no choice but to obey the law of gravity and fall to the sand.

His downward motion had been suddenly arrested, however, by the viselike grip that held his neck. With a single, terrible crack the vertebrae snapped. Then she had released the hold, and his lifeless body dropped to the sand. His muscles had vibrated for a moment in a high-frequency tremor, and one of his legs had made a single, convulsive kick. Then he had lain still.

Kara had stepped easily away from him and shut her eyes, as if in meditation. In fact, she had been experiencing the sensations of pleasure that radiated warmly throughout her body.

She had not been used as a guinea pig again.

When her group of seventeen commandos had elected its leader, she was the one chosen. And when, in the tradition of the camps, the weakest one was put to death by the strongest—barehanded, in unarmed combat—it was she who had performed the task.

Willingly.

Now, as she prepared to sleep, Kara again used her fingertips to trace the scar on her face.

It ran in a thin line along the edge of her jaw, following the jawbone. The mark was on the right side of her face, a faint seam that started beneath her ear and extended to her chin. One of the rapists had done it during the struggle, had made a wild swipe with a razor-sharp blade as she had almost pulled free.

It hadn't hurt at all, not at first, anyway.

Instead it had just felt cold, like ice. And then they had caught her and knocked her into merciful unconsciousness before they finished their assault of her body and her privacy.

Whether they left her for dead, or just didn't care, she did not know. But she had in fact survived, and the cut had healed leaving the faint scar.

Still, at times like this, she would reach around with her left hand and trace the hairline groove. She felt at peace with the world, at peace with herself, knowing that she would soon get the chance to use her gift as it was meant to be used.

Gently, Kara shut her eyes and went to sleep.

1

The man in tan gazed through the plate-glass window of the airport terminal. Beyond the glass, the runway lay cold and gray like the surface of an autopsy table. Though it was midmorning, the winter sun managed only a diffused stainless-steel light through the dirty blanket of smog, fog and haze that covered the Los Angeles International Airport.

A DC-10, ponderous and ungainly on the ground, made its way from the landing strip to the terminal.

Inside the building, near Gate 52 of LAX, was the usual crowd of arriving and departing passengers. Many looked like business or professional people, dressed in suits and wearing expressions of tolerant fatigue. Some were families, an assortment of the young and the old. A few were obviously military personnel, judging by their uniforms and unique haircuts.

A very few were airline personnel catching a flight home or to some other destination.

The families, for the most part, wore looks of excitement. The military types, especially the young ones, had that look of uncertainty that goes with being in a new role. And the airline people simply looked bored, as if they'd already seen enough airline terminals.

Overlying it all came the frequent squawk-box announcements of the airport PA system.

It was late January. The holidays were far enough behind to be only memories, yet it was still two or three months until spring, even in Southern California.

The man in tan gazed through the glass wall for a few moments longer, then sidled away. He drifted to what he determined was the safest place in that part of the terminal.

Safest for somebody in his profession, that is.

It was a spot where the wall was at his back. Moreover, he had a view of both the large room where the passengers waited to board and the corridor that led from that room to the baggage claim area.

He didn't have to consciously select the spot. He didn't even think about what he was doing when he chose it. The act came automatically, the result of long practice reinforced by the notion that he might as well make it as tough as possible for them to get him.

The survival instinct, in other words—Slip up and you're apt to be dead, pal. It had been a powerful incentive to form just such habits.

In most respects, the man in tan was perhaps the least noticeable person in the crowd, at least to the casual observer.

He was in his mid-thirties. He had brown hair and blue eyes. The hair was short and parted on the left, most of it combed over to the right side of his head. He had regular, clean features in a regular, slightly squarish face. His jaw was strong but not angular or jutting. On this occasion, he wore brown-rimmed glasses.

Mr. Average was what he looked like. But as he himself would have readily acknowledged, looks can be deceiving. Especially in his business.

At five-ten and one seventy or so, the man looked fit, although he lacked the muscular bulk of a weight lifter or the lean and drawn appearance of some running addicts. If he had been wearing a business suit, he could have passed as an attorney with a major law firm or a rising corporate executive type.

He was not wearing a suit, however.

His slacks were khaki-tan, stylishly pleated in the front. He wore a brown Members Only jacket. It hung just below his belt line and had epaulets on the shoulders. Beneath the jacket he wore a casual off-white knit shirt.

The overall effect of the man's appearance was slightly rumpled; few would give him a second look.

A very discerning eye, especially one with an artistic bent, might see him as a sort of study in tans, the tan man. But even that eye probably would remember the colors more than the man. Most people wouldn't even notice him at all.

That was exactly what he wanted.

Tucked into the waistband of his trousers, just back of his right hip, was a .45 Government Model semiautomatic pistol. The casual jacket he wore concealed it.

On the outside, the weapon looked like a standard military item, the "knock you down and jump on you" .45 ACP pistol familiar to all U.S. soldiers. Inside, however, the weapon had received special attention in certain minor yet significant aspects.

The magazine had been modified by the addition of a special spring and floor plate, to allow it to hold eight rounds instead of the standard seven. Add one in the chamber, and it meant nine altogether.

One school of thought said that if you can't do it in eight, you probably can't do it in nine, either. Another school said that when your gun locks open and empty, and the other asshole is still on his feet and trying to kill you, you'd sell your old lady's ass for just one more round.

The man in tan didn't know if he'd go that far, but as long as he had the option for another round, he'd take it.

In other respects, certain mechanical parts of the pistol had been the subject of a little buffing here, a little smoothing there, and a slightly different spring somewhere else. All these tasks had been performed by a master weaponsmith known to his friends and close associates simply as the Cowboy.

The tan man at the air terminal was one of those friends and close associates.

The .45 he carried—and had gotten through the airline security due to the credentials he had with him—was nothing more than one of the basic tools of his trade. He had no reason to expect trouble at the terminal—quite the contrary, in fact. But, in his business one generally didn't venture forth without at least the most basic protective weapon, the .45.

"Survival enhancement implements," he liked to call them. He would wink when he said it, but his tone was wry, a grim reminder of what his business was all about.

The nature of that business gave him good reason for being so cautious. Whatever characteristics of the work attracted him to it, the prospects for survival were not among them.

The business was terrorism. Or, in his case, counterterrorism.

The man was one of a small and elite circle of specialists who waged a secret war. The public is aware of some of them, and completely unaware of others. The better-known examples of the species include Delta Force and, from the past, Blue Light, two antiterrorist squads operated by the U.S. government.

This man, and his partners, formed their own kind of Delta Force. They were not formally attached in any permanent or official way to any government department or agency. Instead, they were almost freelancers, working on a case-by-case basis.

Virtually all of their work these days, of course, came from the government.

Cases that made the headlines—the hijacked airline kind of case—went to Delta Force or some equally high-profile group. The ones that didn't make headlines were apt to go to the men of less visible organizations.

Even in Washington, D.C., most of the politicians and policy-makers didn't know about them. They knew that such groups existed, of course, but they didn't know of the specific operation that the man in tan was a part of. Or else they didn't like to admit it.

And, if one of them did know a bit more than his colleagues, even he wouldn't know the details, let alone who were the agents.

"That Stoney Man bunch, or whatever it is," he might say. He would say it in a hushed voice to a trusted colleague, with both secrecy and reverence in his tone.

"Who?" The colleague would feign ignorance, of course. He would sound disapproving that America would countenance the existence of such groups.

"You know," the first official would rejoin, "those fellows that Justice uses from time to time."

"Oh, yeah. I've heard about groups like that." The man would let out a ragged sigh. "I suppose they're necessary, of course, but..."

The ritual expressions of disapproval out of the way, the two officials would get down to business. Often as not, feelers would be put out, feelers that would lead to another mission for the man who now waited at the airport.

The man in tan was part of "that Stony Man bunch," part of a detail known to insiders as Able Team.

Secretive, mobile and deadly, the team moved through the cracks of society. They worked the lowlands, so to speak, combatting twentieth-century terrorists. It became search and destroy at its most dangerous, the rooting out of those wanton individuals who believed in the slaughter of random innocents as a tool of political pressure.

But as Gadgets Schwarz once observed, "It's not particularly lucrative, and the prospects of longevity aren't so hot, either. Still, the work's rewarding and you get to travel a lot."

His audience at the time had been his two friends and partners, an ex-policeman named Carl Lyons and a former Black Beret normally referred to simply as the Politician. Together, the three of them formed perhaps the most effective counterterrorist unit operating in the United States.

Lyons, the ex-cop, was a man not given to understatement. His rejoinder had been more direct. "You mean we get paid shit for chasing all over the country and getting our asses shot off, but it's worth it to get the chance to blow away a few terrorist assholes along the way," he said.

"Basically, yes," agreed the first man, the one now waiting in the terminal.

The man knew it was scarcely his place to dispute the translation. On one of their missions, Lyons had, in fact, been wounded in the particular portion of his anatomy just described.

True, it had only been a neat through-and-through drilling of one cheek by a jacketed bullet. No part had actually been "shot off." Still, the episode made Lyons the undisputed authority on the subject.

Now, as he surveyed the bleak gray of the concrete landing strip, the man in the air terminal thought again of the stainless-steel top of a morgue table.

If that was what the runway resembled, he thought, then the plane looked in some ways like the table's reluctant occupant. The long shape and slow, ungainly movements of the DC-10 created the sudden image of a corpse struggling with stiffening limbs to roll away from the pathologist's knife.

The image disturbed him a little.

However, even as the comparison struck him, another part of his mind—probably the logical left brain—took over. That's enough, Hermann, it told him, in about the same tone his mother would have used. No sense in getting too morbid about these matters.

Easy for you to say, the right side shot back.

A genius with an IQ that ran off the scale, the brain of the man in tan never slowed down. As a kid, he had been an electronics nut, a tinkerer, back when computers were in their infancy. It had been those interests that led to his nickname of Gadgets, to which he answered far more readily than his given name, Hermann Schwarz.

As the computer age exploded, Gadgets had stayed one step ahead of it. And, in a manner unique to true geniuses, his remarkable brain was as open to the imaginative as it was to the technical.

Sometimes, the imaginative part found outlet in humor; he was an inveterate jokester. On a more serious note, however, he had learned that a feeling like the one he now experienced often proved to be a premonition of sorts, a kind of extrasensory foresight. It was a sense that had panned out in an uncanny number of cases.

If that's what this image is, he thought, it can only mean one thing.

Death, in one form or another.

He glanced around the terminal, trying to look casual yet scrutinizing the crowd carefully.

Nothing seemed amiss, nothing out of the ordinary. Passengers hurried to and from the gates. Airline personnel moved from one place to another. A couple of men in work clothes were dismantling one of the television monitors that displayed flight schedules. Orange traffic cones on the floor diverted the flow of passengers around them.

No threat there.

He scanned the rest of the multitude. Security was tight in these days of terrorist bombings and attacks, and the crowd appeared to be the normal assortment of travelers.

Maybe the danger came from elsewhere, assuming it was a danger and not just an overactive imagination.

He glanced at the bleak gray runway. There was the plane, still swinging stiffly around. To one side stood a tank truck and a squat baggage cart, both empty.

There was nothing but empty runway in the other direction.

Nothing out there resembled danger.

Then, and only then, did the man in tan relax and allow himself to listen to the other voice in his mind, the one that said he was just being morbid. After all, Gadgets told himself, not every vague feeling of disquiet meant trouble.

Hell, maybe he was just hungry, he thought. Or, more precisely, he knew he was hungry, and maybe that was all it was, the low-blood-sugar blues.

Gadgets imagined that inside the plane, the stewardess—make that "flight attendant," he corrected himself—would be reminding the passengers to remain seated until the aircraft came to a complete stop. And, if things were running true to form, the passengers would be ignoring her.

Finally, the plane halted some twenty yards away. Then it began a slow pivot around the left wheel, causing the nose to swing up to the end of the portable tunnel that dangled out from the terminal like some great tentacle. Minutes later, the passengers began to emerge from the tunnel into the terminal.

Eyes probing the stream of humanity, Gadgets looked for his passenger.

He knew her from an earlier mission. An agent with the FBI, named Julie Harris. Thick, dark hair. Good-looking in a strong, vital sort of way. And, she happened to be the girlfriend of Carl Lyons, his Able Team partner and friend.

Lyons was unavailable, and Gadgets had volunteered to meet her at the airport.

Her being in town was, Gadgets surmised, part business and part pleasure. He knew she had to check in with her own agency, at the Bureau's L.A. field office. He also knew she wanted to see Lyons ASAP—or at least, Lyons wanted to see her, and he guessed the feeling was mutual.

But that wasn't the only reason she was coming there, Gadgets suspected, and it probably wasn't the main reason. There had to be something else, some other mission.

All the indicators said so.

It had been Able Team's own boss, Hal Brognola, who had informed them of Julie's arrival. The chief had called them the preceding day. He had made the call from their headquarters at Stony Man Farm, in the mountains of Virginia not far from Washington, D.C., to let them know when and where she was arriving.

Make sure somebody is there to meet her, he had said.

That was, to say the least, highly unusual.

Brognola did not work for the FBI any more than Gadgets or Lyons or the Politician did. The FBI did its thing, which was investigating federal crimes and holding press conferences, and the Stony Man crew did theirs. And, although the goal was the same, the similarity ended with that.

Operationally speaking, the two groups couldn't have been less similar.

The Bureau was far superior to other organizations when it came to putting together cases for prosecution. This was especially so in sophisticated fraud and corruption matters. Its targets were carefully and conservatively chosen, its methods above reproach and its results excellent. Gadgets knew that and respected the fact, notwithstanding the occasional case where a criminal and his attorney managed to con a judge and jury into believing he'd been entrapped.

Stony Man had no inclination toward doing the Bureau's job. Brognola and his boys normally couldn't care less about prosecution. Or entrapment either, for that matter. Rather, their forte was more directly remedial.

Quite bluntly, as Lyons would have put it, "I hope to hell we entrap 'em. That's the whole idea. Hunt the bastards down, entrap 'em, and put 'em away for good."

Most of the FBI had no inkling that Stony Man existed. And the only times the members of the two groups ever worked together were on an ad hoc, case-by-case basis. Usually, it meant the legal means had proved ineffective, or the urgency was so immediate that extraordinary methods were condoned.

And Stony Man's methods were, to say the least, extraordinary.

Accordingly, when Brognola made contact to tell them that Julie would be coming to Los Angeles, and that one of them should meet her, Gadgets wondered if something were up. Of course, his suspicions could have been the result of professional paranoia or an overactive imagination. Or maybe he had merely been hungry then, too.

It could even be that Brognola had made the request simply as a favor to Lyons. The chief knew, of course, that Lyons and Julie were involved in some sort of relationship. But somehow that didn't seem quite right.

Oh, well, he thought as he scanned the passengers, we'll soon know. For now, the game plan was to locate her and play taxi. And, of course, get something to eat—he was even starting to crave some of Lyons's cooking. And that meant the situation was a red alert.

He sidled over to get a better look at the deplaning travelers.

She wasn't the first one off, or the second one. Or the third or tenth or twentieth, either. Ignoring his growling stomach, Gadgets waited.

Finally, just at that point when he was starting to wonder if she had made the flight, he saw her. She was just coming around a bend far down the tunnel, a briefcase in one hand. As she neared the mouth of the ramp, a small knot of radically dressed rock-singer types jostled her from behind. They pushed past her, and for a moment, she was hidden from sight behind them.

Then he saw her again.

Through a gap above people's shoulders and between their heads, Gadgets saw her eyes probing the crowd, a dark, beautiful woman with a permanent air of mystery to her. Her eyes met his, and she smiled and altered her course to come toward him.

The image of death welled up again. Angrily, he forced it away, pushed it down and out of his mind.
Too late, he realized what it meant.

2

The man in tan was not the only man with a mission at LAX that day. Near the gate sat another man who was acutely interested in the arriving passengers.

He didn't show his interest however. And he certainly did not reveal *why* he was interested.

A superficial look conveyed that he was a salesman, perhaps, or a schoolteacher or some kind of coach. He had on a blue L.A. Dodgers baseball cap, with dark blue polyester slacks and a dress shirt of very pale yellow. He was wearing a tie with stripes that alternated between dark blue, light blue and tan. Over the shirt he wore a nylon jacket. The jacket was that bright color that L.A. fans refer to as "Dodger blue."

He carried what is sometimes called a catalog case.

The case sat at his feet as he waited in the metal and plastic airport seat. It was not an attaché case, exactly, but a sort of oversize rectangular briefcase made of a hard material. An ordinary briefcase would just fit inside it, in fact.

That was exactly what the man in Dodger blue intended.

If one took a careful look at him, the man didn't really resemble a salesman or teacher or coach. He had unusually pale skin. Although not everybody in Southern California has a beach tan, this man wasn't even close. His features suggested that he was eastern European or perhaps Slavic.

But it wasn't the man's pale skin or his nationality that took him out of the running for being a teacher or salesman. Instead, the difference lay in his eyes and the expression on his face.

The face was that of a taker, not a giver. Had Gadgets, or either of his partners, for that matter, been given a look at the man, the recognition would have been instantaneous.

He was a killer.

It wouldn't be that the Able Team personnel knew this particular man, or would recognize him. It would simply be that they knew the type.

The man watched and waited quietly. He smoked a cigarette and blew the gray plumes of smoke toward the ceiling. From where he sat, he had a view of the entire waiting area, from the mouth of the tunnel to the men working on the TV monitor in the coned-off area.

His facial muscles betrayed his tension, however.

There was no nervous tic, no fidgeting or blinking. Instead, the man's nerves were betrayed by the opposite type of signs—his features were frozen and immobile, held rigid by the tense muscles beneath the skin. Indeed, a careful observer would have noted that the man's whole body looked inflexible. Even the motion of raising the cigarette to his lips seemed mechanical, robotlike.

Nobody, however, looked that carefully.

Nobody saw the tension, or the bulge under the left arm that signified a 9 mm semiautomatic pistol. The handgun was a standard Smith & Wesson Model 59, which held thirteen rounds of the hot 9 mm Parabellum.

The pistol had one nonstandard feature, however.

The barrel had been changed. The factory tube had been removed and another virtually identical one had been put in its place. The difference between the standard item and the replacement lay in the rifling, the grooves that ran the length of the barrel on the inside to make the bullet spin.

Most handguns had six parallel grooves that twisted their way along the inside of the barrel. This one had four.

The four twisted to the right, in a ratio of one complete turn to ten inches, although of course the barrel length on the Model 59 was nowhere near ten inches.

Four grooves, right-hand twist, one-in-ten, happened to be the configuration of the rifling on Uzi assault rifles and pistols. The Model 59's rifling had been modified to approximate that of an Uzi, even down to the widths of the lands and grooves.

The result was that a 9 mm slug fired from this pistol would not look as if it came from a Smith & Wesson. If such a bullet were recovered intact—if it had been fired into the soft tissue of a person's abdomen or neck and hadn't hit bone—it would appear to have come from an Uzi.

If luck had it that somebody else on the scene was firing an Uzi, this modified Smith & Wesson would confuse the issue when the FBI's forensic experts were sorting out the bodies and reconstructing the scene.

True, it wasn't foolproof.

The extractor markings on the spent shells would be different, for instance. But it would be confusing, and confusion was the favorite tactic of defense attorneys, should things go to hell and end up in a criminal prosecution. It would all help to raise that magical "reasonable doubt" to justify an acquittal in the minds of a judge or jury.

The man in Dodger blue knew this was a very minor detail in the grand scheme of things, but he believed in being careful.

Very careful, in fact.

He believed that if a hit were planned down to such minute details as trying to confuse firearms identification experts, the chances of something going wrong were fewer. In other words, he knew that the big details had been handled if they were planning such sophisticated and minor tactics.

The man lit another cigarette from the butt of his last one. Then the first persons to leave the plane—two airline employees who had probably wanted to hop another flight home—appeared in the tunnel.

The man stubbed out the cigarette he had just lit.

He got to his feet and looked around. Then he picked up his catalog case and drifted away from the mouth of the tunnel.

Some fifteen feet to the right of the gate was a counter and computer terminal where boarding passes were issued. The man found a spot behind it. He leaned against the wall and waited.

Most of the waiting area was now behind him, hidden from his view. He could no longer see the orange cones around where the men were fixing the television monitor, nor the hallways that led to the baggage claim area.

But he could see what he needed to see. He could see the deplaning passengers. And he was protected from the field of fire by the counter.

He watched and waited as the passengers began to emerge.

It seemed to him as if most of them must have gotten off. Then the shooting started—automatic weapons fire, Uzi 9 mms—and the passengers began to come apart in a spray of blood and bits of tissue.

3

A single shrill scream echoed in the crowded terminal. It came from a woman in her forties, a pleasant-looking motherly type, whom fate had placed closest to the gunman.

Then, abruptly, it stopped short, chopped by the hammering explosions of the automatic weapons wielded by the two killers.

The woman spun around and sprawled onto the tiled floor, leaving a slick streak of red on the shiny finish. For a brief moment, nobody else screamed, or yelled. The only sounds were the rapid-fire blasts of gunfire.

During that instant, the crowd seemed to hold its collective breath.

The travelers froze in stunned silence. Then, like a dam that finally gives way to release a massive wall of water, the silence broke in a torrent of shrieks and screams. Terrified people scrambled in all directions, their common purpose being to get away from the line of destruction that lay before the guns.

It was a line that ran from the muzzles of the gun barrels to the mouth of the tunnel where passengers were disembarking.

The killers, two men with bushy black hair and mustaches and a vaguely Middle Eastern cast to them, moved away from the coned-off area where they had been working on the television monitor. Knees slightly bent, each with an assault rifle clamped against his side, they moved forward, directing sweeps of gunfire toward the terrified crowd.

Gadgets reacted immediately. Without conscious thought, he moved into action. Crouching, he spun around to face the danger, to move into a position to "neutralize the threat," as it was sometimes phrased.

To blow the assholes away, in other words.

Even as he swung around, however, he knew with a sickening certainty who the target had to be. Coincidences did happen, of course, and terrorists were likely to strike at any time or place. Still, in his heart, Gadgets knew that this was not some random attack where some FBI agent by chance was in the field of fire.

She was dead, and he knew it.

He knew it as certainly as if he had seen her take the hits, and had examined the body afterward.

Julie would have just been at the mouth of the tunnel, at the top of the inclined ramp, when the shooting started. She wouldn't be the only victim, of course—the rock-singer types who had jostled by her would die also, as would many other innocents, men, women and children alike.

But she was the target.

In that split second, he understood it. It all made sense. Brognola's calling them to meet her at the airport—it must have been because Julie had some important information she was bringing to them. And the images of death—his own morbid vision of the approaching plane being a corpse on an autopsy table, the resulting feeling of disquiet, of apprehension—he understood as well.

His imagery had not been wrong. He himself had been at fault for doubting it.

He knew all this in the single instant that the gunfire erupted. And then, the only thing left to do was salvage what could be salvaged.

If anything.

As his friend Carl Lyons would put it, "If you can't stop the breakage, at least break the breakers."

Time to break 'em.

The gunmen were still firing. The racket was deafening, the shots ringing above the sounds of the crowd's panic. Thin gray smoke from the smokeless powder began to drift in narrow eddies from the guns. The acrid, chemical scent of burned ordnance hung in the air.

It was 9 mm, he knew from the sound. The weapons would be Uzis, most likely, or one of the many imitations thereof. Thirty-two round magazine, probably. He heard the momentary pause as one of the weapons emptied. It was followed immediately by the telltale metallic click-clack of the clip being twisted out and another slapped into place.

It'll be getting hot, he thought.

As he moved forward, Gadgets's mind was working, sifting, shifting, all the time in the combat mode. He knew the area by the gun's breach would be too hot to touch. The terrorist would be well advised to start firing shorter bursts rather than sustained fire.

He wondered if the gunman knew that.

The answer came a moment later. The gunfire took on an intermittent character, short, deadly bursts of autoburn rather than continuous fire.

The result was, if anything, more frightening than the earlier sustained fire.

Gadgets's hand flashed to his side, behind the right hip, where the .45 rode inside his trousers. Then the brutelike pistol was in his hand. He held it inconspicuously down by his thigh, muzzle pointed at the floor, and then he was moving forward, angling ahead to try to get a shot at the gunmen.

However harmless he might have looked moments before, in that instant he, too, became in many ways like the gunmen. He was a stone killer, a pro about to do what he was a pro at doing.

A screaming woman ran into him as she plunged blindly away from the killers. She was overweight, and the impact knocked him backward and half spun him around. Gadgets swore and shoved her to one side as he tried to forge ahead. All around him the crowd surged like white-water rapids, and for a moment he thought it was a lost cause.

Then one of the terrorists helped him.

Their main work done, Gadgets figured, the two killers turned their attention elsewhere. They did this by raking the crowd with gunfire, to give the appearance that the attack was a random terrorist episode. Then, they did a very un-terrorist thing.

They turned around to run.

That act registered in the mind of the Able Team genius immediately. He filed it away for future reference.

In a grim sort of way, the killers' last sweep of gunfire helped Gadgets. It mowed down several people in the crowd that had been buffeting him and preventing him from getting a clear path to his targets. As the muzzle-flashes and the thundering firepower swept his way, those people who weren't hit fell to the floor, scrambling away from the killers.

Suddenly, he was the only one left standing in the immediate area. The others were either hit or cowering on the floor.

Gadgets's compendious mind had always been able to work on several levels at the same time. But even as he grimly stalked toward the two gunmen, a memory flashed into part of his consciousness.

It was a scene from his childhood.

He had been on a hunting trip as a youth, engaging in the time-honored boyhood activity of hunting quail and rabbits in the brushy desert wasteland north of Los Angeles. A jackrabbit had appeared ahead of him, and had begun running diagonally up a sandy embankment.

The jack blasted up the slope, its powerful hindquarters propelling it forward with bursts of power. It was an almost impossible target, even given the close range, due to its jerky speed.

The young Gadgets and his boyhood friend, Tony Anthony, had both been carrying shotguns. Gadget's had been a Remington pump, a Model 870 in twelve gauge. He had fired three quick shots at the fleeing rabbit, but had missed with all three, each one kicking up a puff of dust and dirt in the wake of the fleeing creature.

Then the jack had frozen beyond a dry, scrubby bush a couple of feet high. Instinct had apparently told it to conceal itself behind the low plant.

Instinct had very nearly proved to be wrong—dead wrong—for the jack on that day.

The boy's next blast had all but vaporized the bush. The fine birdshot in the shot shell had shredded the brittle, dry plant, exploding it into nothingness. However, the sandlike pellets themselves had not penetrated to hit the scrawny rabbit beyond it.

In a way, it had been funny.

At "time one" the rabbit had been crouched behind a bush concealed from them, and probably feeling safe.

At "time two," an instant later, the bush had vanished, disintegrated. There was a dramatic illustration of the difference between cover and concealment—the former stopped bullets as well as vision; the latter stopped vision only.

Neither youth had fired at the crouched rabbit.

"Git!" Gadgets had finally shouted, waving his arms. The jack took off, unharmed, to live to run another day. It had been through enough, they reasoned, and deserved the break.

Today, in a sense, Gadgets was in the position of the jackrabbit.

At "time one," he was surrounded by people. At "time two," an instant later, he was the only one standing before the gunmen.

Unlike the jackrabbit, however, Gadgets did not run. He did not want to run; the thought never entered his mind.

Nor did he give the gunmen another chance, as he had given the rabbit.

The closest killer, the one whose 9 mm had raked beyond where Gadgets was standing, had turned to flee. Apparently he glimpsed or sensed the danger, and looked back. The man's eyes widened uncomprehendingly, a combination of shocked surprise and maybe even a little fear.

Gadgets could read it in the eyes. Here is somebody who didn't fall to the floor like the rest of them, the eyes said. And he has a gun in his hand.

The man looked shocked, indignant almost. It was as if he thought Gadgets weren't playing fair. After all, in America, when you pull out automatic weapons in an airport and start shooting, there aren't supposed to be people there to shoot back.

Good, thought Gadgets. I want the bastard to know he's going to die.

The terrorist recovered and swung the Uzi to bear on the man in tan.

Boom!

The .45 made a deeper, more authoritative sound than the heavy clatter of the 9 mm that the Uzi fired. A moment later—just enough time that a bystander might have wondered if another shot were going to be fired—a second boom echoed above the screams of the crowd.

Gadgets fired both shots by instinct and a skill born of endless hours of training.

No cop-approved, two-handed grip, where the left hand cups under the heel of the right one, the two arms making a bipod of sorts. No aiming even. Just a quick, seemingly easy snap shot—raise the arm up and shoot when it was the right time.

Then shift over to the other man and do the same thing.

All the time Gadgets looked at his targets, first one man, and then the other. He didn't even see the .45 in his own hand, let alone use the sights. The gun it was just there. Instead, he kept his gaze on the men themselves, and shot when it felt right. The .45 became an extension of his eye and his hand.

Two shots, in about the time that it takes to say "one-potato-two."

And, watching the men rather than his gun, Gadgets saw them die.

The first man took the round just to one side of his nose. The pathologist who did the autopsies would later report that the impact of the massive, silver-tip slug had shattered the jawbone and smashed the jaw's hinge out of place on that side. The bullet had then ripped through the skull into the brainpot, and had torn a chunk of bone the size of a twenty-five-cent piece from the back of the cranium as it exited.

The second man, the pathologist would report, had taken the shot a little lower, dead center in the case of the neck. It had blown a section of spine out of the back of his neck. To be precise, one vertebra and parts of two more were gone.

Death was instantaneous in each case.

Casually, Gadgets lowered the pistol and pushed back into the crowd. Inside five seconds, the .45 was back in place, and he was moving through the turmoil of humanity, first ten and then fifteen feet away from where he had fired the shots.

More to the point, he was away from the people who had been close enough to see him do the shooting.

The glasses came off—he didn't need them, anyway—and he made his way through the melee to where the deplaning victims had fallen.

He found her easily. One look confirmed what he already knew.

Julie's face was unmarked, even peaceful. Her eyes were closed, as if in sleep. But the front of her dress was soaked—drenched—with blood, and Gadgets could see the cruel, craterlike entrance wounds in her torso. He saw five of them, one of which looked as if two shots had struck virtually the same spot.

She had never had a chance. He crouched quickly and touched her face, feeling at the base of her neck for the pulse he knew he wouldn't find.

Suddenly, her eyes flickered open.

For a moment, they were wide and staring. Then they came to a tight focus on his face.

He bent over her. "Julie?" His voice was low and urgent. "Julie, do you hear me?"

The facial muscles around her eyes were the first to move, as she tried to speak through the shock. Then her lips moved and when she spoke to him in a low, clear voice, he was surprised at how strong it sounded. She said in a single word.

"Powers."

For perhaps once in his life, Gadgets did not know what to do.

"What, Julie?"

A paroxysm of coughing hit her. She choked and hacked, expelling a gout of bright red arterial blood onto his arm. When the cough subsided, she spoke again, this time in a hoarse whisper.

"Axis Powers," she repeated. Her gaze fell to the blood on his coat sleeve. "Sorry, Gadg," she whispered.

He started to speak, to say something idiotic like, "don't worry about it," but she looked up at his eyes again. In an effort of great pain, her lips moved.

"Tell Carl..." she began.

She never finished the sentence. Her voice simply halted. Her eyes lost their focus, and her body seemed to subside a little in his arms, so that she somehow looked smaller in death than she had in life.

Gadgets the friend let Gadgets the pro take over.

He laid her gently back on the floor. Then he took hold of the briefcase she had been carrying and stood up. Unhurriedly, he melted into the turmoil of the crowd, away from the sad, still form on the floor.

4

Gadgets left LAX, caught the freeway south and then took the first off ramp. The ramp ran downhill in a long straight slope, parallel to the freeway. At the bottom, it intersected a surface street, which to the left ran under the freeway and to the right disappeared into the seemingly endless L.A. sprawl.

The Able Team warrior stopped at the stop sign at the bottom of the ramp—last thing in the world he wanted right then was a face-to-face with one of L.A.'s finest over a traffic ticket—then he turned right on the surface street. After that, he made an immediate left into the lot of a Standard gas station and found the pay phone.

Three vehicles behind Gadget's rented sedan was a blue van.

The van had followed him from the airport. During the short freeway ride, it had stayed behind him, one lane over. As Gadgets took the off ramp, the van slid skillfully over and followed suit. So well-practiced was the maneuver that no telltale honk issued from any of the other motorists on the road.

Had Gadgets seen the van, he would have noted that it, too, turned right at the bottom of the ramp.

Instead of following him into the Standard station, however, the van made another right and pulled into the lot of a Denny's restaurant across the street. It made a slow circuit of the lot until it was again facing the street. Then it drove slowly into a parking space next to the exit of the lot.

Nobody got out of the van, however.

Again, had Gadgets been aware of the van, he might have observed it parking. He might also have seen that a curtain—two curtains, actually—hung down from the van's ceiling, directly behind the front seats. Thus, somebody looking into the driver's area from outside of the van, could not see into the rear portion of the interior.

The curtains met in the center of the van, between the two front bucket seats.

Gadgets didn't see any of this. He didn't see the van, and he didn't see the man.

The man, however, saw Gadgets.

The man in Dodger blue removed the ignition keys and surveyed the situation for a moment. Then he nodded to himself, and crawled through the space between the seats to the back of the van. He pulled the curtains shut behind him, leaving a gap of perhaps three or four inches where the heavy fabric met.

Once in the rear of the van, the driver opened a folding camp stool and set it behind the gap in the curtain. Then he removed a pair of powerful binoculars from a briefcase that had been lying on the van's floor. Positioning himself on the stool, he adjusted the baseball cap on his head so the bill wouldn't be in his way, and lifted the binoculars to his eyes.

For several long moments he gazed through the field glasses at the man using the pay phone.

No doubt about it.

It was definitely the same one who had been at the airport, the one who had killed the two gunmen and taken the broad's briefcase, the briefcase he had been sent to get.

That wasn't good.

Whoever this guy was, he *was* good, thought the man in Dodger blue. It was time to take some action, to make a report, get some backup.

He reached between the curtain and opened a wooden case that had been mounted between the bucket seats. Inside was a mobile telephone. He pushed some buttons, paused, listened, then pushed some more buttons.

Finally, a familiar voice came on the line.

"Yeah?"

"Get me Vince," said the man in Dodger blue. He was back to sitting on the folding stool, holding the field glasses to his eyes with one hand and the phone to his ear in the other.

"Rafe? That you? What the fuck took you so long to call? You know—"

"Get me Vince, goddammit!"

"Aw right, aw right. Just hang on a fuckin' minute, will ya? An' Rafe, this better be good."

The man in Dodger blue—Rafe—snarled his reply. "Get me Vince, and now, or I'll cut your heart out when I get back."

A moment later another voice came on the line. This one was professional, composed. He didn't waste time by declaring that the information had better be good, or by asking why Rafe had taken so long to call. It wasn't that this man, Vince, was easygoing, or that he wasn't concerned with these matters. It was simply that he knew those things could wait.

"This is Vince."

"Vince, Rafe. Things have gone to shit."

"How so?" inquired the smooth voice. "The radio just said they had an unconfirmed report of a massacre at the airport."

"They had a massacre, all right. But—"

"Did they get the broad?" interrupted Vince calmly. "Did you get the report?"

"We got the broad, but... we didn't get the report."

The man with the smooth voice hesitated slightly before making his reply. That scared Rafe, even though Rafe himself was the mob's best killer, a hit man who never missed.

If almost anybody else threatened him, directly—even, say, came right out and said, "Rafe, I'm gonna kill ya"—he'd laugh in the guy's face.

But Vince... well, Vince was different.

Vince Danelli was perhaps the only man on earth Rafe feared. And to anybody who knew Rafe, that meant Vince had to be one mean motherfucker.

Rafe had served in Vietnam. He had barely escaped being court-martialed for his role in some particularly gruesome atrocities, in which he and another Marine had tried to determine the best place to stab people to kill them. Their subjects had been live Vietcong, captured in various sorties.

Rafe had earned the reputation for being as tough and competent as he was cruel.

Danelli was even worse. And, to Rafe's mind, a lot more scary. The madder Vince got, the calmer he sounded. And when Vince Danelli, the most trusted lieutenant in the Chicago Mafia, got mad, somebody usually died. Rafe knew that he, himself, was tough. And he also knew that Vince, despite his executive level status with the Mafia, was tougher.

"What happened, Rafe?" came Vince's voice, still low and even.

Rafe switched to a more respectful form of addressing the man on the other end of the line.

"The two dudes made the hit like clockwork, Mr. Danelli. Shot the shit outta the broad, and mowed down a whole bunch of other people besides. You know, to make it look just like a routine terrorist attack."

"Yes."

"Then they start movin', just like they was supposed to, to draw people away from the broad. Move the action, like we talked about."

"So why didn't you get the papers, Rafe?"

"There was this guy there, see."

"What guy, Rafe? A Feebie?"

"No. Least, I don't think he was a Feeb. He's gotta be government somehow, but he don't look like Bureau."

"So what did this guy do, Rafe?"

"This guy was there, waitin' for her. Ordinary-lookin' dude, just a guy in the crowd. Not wearin' a suit or nothing." Rafe paused, not wanting to get into the bad news, and hoping he would get some encouraging indicator from Vince.

He didn't. Finally, he went on.

"This guy comes out of nowhere, see. He's some totally nondescript fuckin' nobody in the crowd. Next thing you know, he's got a .45 in his hand and he's somehow movin' in on the gunners."

"And?"

Rafe couldn't ever remember Vince sounding so expressionless. "An' he takes 'em out. Two shots. One each. Head shots. I never seen anythin' like it, boss. Poof, he's just fuckin' there, like outta thin air. Then, Bang! Bang! Just like pointin' your finger."

"He got both of them?"

"Sure did, boss. He—"

"*Both* of them?"

"Head shots, like I said. With a .45. And the next thing I know, he's over by the broad, tryin' to talk to her. And then he takes the briefcase and splits."

"He got the briefcase?"

"Yeah, boss. Like I said—"

"I heard you." Vince's voice snapped like a whip. "Where were you?"

"Boss, I—"

"Skip it."

Rafe realized that for the first time he could remember, Vince actually sounded irritated. Then a sudden panic struck him. Usually, the madder Vince got the quieter he got. What if this meant he had gone beyond any previous stage of anger? What if the failure of this caper had pushed Vince to a level of anger he had never reached before, one where he actually showed it?

The thought terrified him.

Rafe knew he might as well put his gun in his own mouth right now, if that were the case. The head-in-the-vise routine would be the best thing he could hope for otherwise.

To distract himself, so he wouldn't dwell on the immediate possibilities, Rafe kept the field glasses focused on the man at the pay phone. Guy's been on the horn for quite a while, he thought. Wait. Now he had started back to his car. But he left the telephone hanging.

Holy shit, now the guy had his .45 out and was gonna blow away some other dirtbag....

Vince's voice interrupted him.

"Rafe. That briefcase had some very important papers in it. We gotta have them. They'll tell us everything the Feebies know about a case we're involved in."

"I know, Vi—"

"*We* gotta know what *they* know about us. We gotta have that file. Now, tell me again. The guy got away with the briefcase? That's what you're telling me?

You're not just being cute, Rafe? You're not thinking of trying to hold us up, are you, Rafe?"

"Th-tha-that's right, Vince—Mr. Danelli," he stuttered. "Honest to God—"

"The guy got away?"

"Yes, but—"

"But what, Rafe?"

"But I followed him." The words tumbled out in a rush. "I followed him, Mr. Danelli. I got him in my sight right now. He's still got the case."

"You followed him? Why didn't you say so?"

"I—"

"Never mind. Where is he?"

"Gas station, foot of the off ramp to Ardan, just south of the airport."

"He alone?"

"Yeah."

"What's he doing, Rafe?"

"He's been talkin' on a pay phone."

"Ardan off ramp, you say, Rafe?"

"That's it, boss."

"Stay on him, Rafe."

"Yes, Mr. Danelli."

"I mean, really stay with him. Stay on him like stink on shit. The boys will be on their way."

"Wha—"

"You and the boys'll kill him. And you'll get the briefcase, like you should have in the first place."

5

Gadgets made the telephone call from a pay telephone at the first off ramp.

The call went through at almost exactly fourteen minutes after he left Julie's side. Gadgets had glanced at his watch after he had lowered her limp body to the floor, and had noted the time.

From the phone booth, though, it took nearly two minutes for the call to go through. Those two minutes—or a hundred and twenty seconds—felt like ten, under the circumstances.

As he waited, Gadgets wondered which president he should thank for allowing the Justice Department to wage its antitrust war against AT&T. Jimmy Carter, probably. The result of that blow for consumer independence was, in Gadgets's estimation, that it only took about three or four times as long to place a long distance call as it had under the big, bad monopoly that used to exist.

Or maybe he was just in a bad mood.

Probably the call only took twice as long as it used to, he thought disgustedly. It was another example of the trouble one gets into when lawyers are allowed to run the show.

He shook his head grimly. What the hell. At this point, another minute or two probably wouldn't make any difference.

It certainly wouldn't matter to Julie, wherever she was now. It didn't matter to the gunmen, for the same reason. And it really didn't affect him, either. He was in a position of relative safety, and didn't need any immediate assistance.

Still, the delay irritated him. The incident at the airport was the sort of thing that should be reported to Brognola ASAP. Especially since Gadgets had helped himself to Julie's briefcase.

Gadgets called direct. He didn't bother to use the secret lines. Nothing he had to say was that secret, and there was no telling how long *that* would have taken.

A voice he didn't recognize answered the phone. "Hello?"

"I need to speak to Mr. Brognola," Gadgets said, surprised that it wasn't Aaron "the Bear" Kurtzman who had answered.

"May I say who is calling?"

"This is Mr. Schwarz. I'm calling from a pay phone. It's important that I get in touch with Mr. Brognola immediately."

"Stand by."

In a moment, Brognola came on the line, his voice booming and reassuring.

"Brognola here."

"This is me, Chief," said Gadgets. "I'm calling from a pay phone, and the line isn't secure."

"Gadgets, me boy!" boomed the chief. "I assumed the line hadn't been cleared, or you wouldn't have been doing the 'Mr. Brognola' number."

"That's right. Where's the Bear? Who answered the phone?"

"Temporary help. Thoroughly cleared, of course. I've got Kurtzman doing other things." He declined to provide further details. "What's up? You sound pissed off."

"I am."

"So, tell me."

"Well, Chief, if you get the Bear cranked up to do the electronic eavesdropping routine for a while—tap into a few official channels—you'll know. Or maybe just turn on the TV, or radio." Even as he spoke, Gadgets could tell his own voice had an uncharacteristically harsh sound to it.

Brognola evidently sensed it. His voice became immediately all business. "Report."

"I wasn't the only welcoming party for flight 187, Chief. Two men with full-auto Uzis staged a party of their own."

"Casualties?" Brognola's voice was flat and emotionless, prepared to hear bad news.

"The max. I didn't stick around to count, but it looked like a bunch of civilians and one lady FBI agent."

Ghost Train

A silence followed this announcement. Finally, the Stony Man leader spoke softly. "You're sure about that?"

His tone indicated he knew Gadgets was sure, but he had to check anyway.

Gadgets swallowed. For all the death he'd seen, including a good bit he'd dealt out himself, the Able Team commando found himself strangely close to tears on this one. Maybe it was because she'd been so brave, yet had looked so vulnerable in death.

He cleared his throat and sought refuge in the emotionless nomenclature used by military and police enterprises everywhere. The terminology had the effect of depersonalizing the death, somehow.

"That's affirmative, Chief."

"Stand by."

Gadgets heard Brognola say something over his shoulder. Though muffled—Gadgets had seen the Chief put his meaty palm over the mouthpiece in the past—it sounded like, "Get Kurtzman."

That would fit, thought Gadgets.

Brognola would be wanting the Bear to check the official channels of communication to intercept any reports on this. Gadgets heard the muffled sound of more instructions being issued, and tried not to think of the woman who had used two of her last four words to apologize for bleeding on his sleeve.

Then Brognola was back on the line. "What happened to the attackers?"

"They died."

"How many did you say there were? Two?"

"Two."

"And both of them died?"

"Yes."

The Stony Man chief apparently knew exactly what his agent meant. "Anybody onto you?"

"Negative. No hot pursuit, anyway. If any of the video cameras happened to catch me, it may be different, of course. Or maybe if some Zapruder-type tourist was shooting home movies. But short of that, you'll probably get fifty different descriptions, all too vague to use."

"Probably. Well, good work on that."

"Yeah. Great."

After a pause, Brognola spoke again. "Are you sure about the agent?"

"She died in my arms, Chief."

"Oh. I see." Brognola's voice was soft. Gadgets wondered if his boss was considering only the tactical ramifications, or if he felt the human loss as well.

"Yeah."

After a moment, Brognola spoke again. "Did she happen to say anything before she died?"

"Yes."

"What?"

"This is an open line, Chief."

"I'm aware of that. What did she say?"

Gadgets closed his eyes. In his mind, he was back there again, some fifteen to eighteen minutes ago.

"She said, 'Powers. Axis Powers,' it sounded like."

"'Powers'?"

"Yes, goddammit. 'Axis Powers.'" Gadgets drew a husky breath, then went on. "Then she... said she was sorry she got blood on my jacket, and she started to tell me to tell Lyons something, only she died halfway through it."

"'Powers'?" Brognola was clearly puzzled.

"That's what it sounded like, Chief. The 'Powers' part I know is correct. The 'Axis' I'm pretty sure of. She was coughing up a lot of blood at the time, but it's hard to figure what else it could be."

"Axis Powers," mused Brognola. "What the hell could that mean?"

Gadgets shook his head, forgetting that Brognola couldn't see him over the telephone. He forced the image of the dead woman out of his mind by searching his compendious memory for the meaning of the term. For some reason, the thought of his tenth-grade history teacher popped up.

Sophomore year was modern world history. Then he had it.

"Axis powers," he repeated. "Wasn't that what they called the countries that were against us in World War II?"

Brognola was ahead of him.

"Yes. Of course." His voice sounded distracted. "Actually, it meant the countries that were allied against the Allies. Nazi Germany and Fascist Italy, to be exact, though later they threw in Japan as well."

"If you knew, why did you ask?" inquired Gadgets, irritated. "With all due respect," he added. Actually, though, he didn't feel particularly respectful to anybody at that moment.

"Of course I knew what the Axis powers were," Brognola snapped. His tone made clear that he was just as irritated. "I just don't see how that fits into the current project."

There it is! thought Gadgets with grim satisfaction.

Unconsciously, he nodded a second time. His chief had hesitated just a fraction before the words "current project." So, the hunch that Gadgets had felt when Brognola first dispatched him to meet Julie at the airport had been right. Something was, in fact, up.

Something was in the wind. Something that involved Able Team.

Something that involved the FBI.

It had to be, because Julie worked for the Bureau, and her first loyalty was there. He corrected himself, *had worked* for the Bureau, that is.

She must have been bringing something for them. That was why it was so imperative that somebody meet her at the airport. And the only way the Bureau could solicit Stony Man's help was to have the requests cleared at the highest levels. It also meant this was going to be a real dirty one.

Something where the nice, civilized, conventional, legal ways had failed.

Something that needed not-so-nice, uncivilized, unconventional, illegal ways in order to succeed.

In short, something for Able Team.

Maybe the nice ways had just proved ineffective. Maybe something had blown up in somebody's face—

figuratively or literally—over it. Maybe a mission had fallen on its own sword. Or maybe it had been killed by the enemy's.

And, it was something Brognola had known about. It had to be. Very likely, he had intended to brief them on it after Julie arrived. And now, he was trying to figure out how the clue she had gasped out fit into what he already knew.

He wasn't having much luck, from the sound of it.

Then Gadgets remembered something.

"One more thing, Chief."

"Yes?" Brognola's voice boomed, but not very genially. Gadgets wondered if it was a mirror of his own mood, or if the Chief was feeling a lot of pressure on this one. Most likely it was both.

"I snagged her briefcase before I got out of there."

There was a moment of stunned silence before Brognola spoke. "Repeat that," he demanded.

Gadgets did.

"What in the hell made you grab her briefcase?"

"Just a hunch." Gadgets didn't feel like explaining further, or going into his precognitive images of the airplane and the autopsy table.

"And you have it with you?"

"That's affirmative."

"Have you looked inside?"

"No."

"Look in it now. See if there's anything that refers to 'Lambda.'"

"'Lambda'?"

"Yes. Like the letter of the Greek alphabet."

"Stand by, Chief." Gadgets left the phone hanging, and started to go to the car, parked only some ten feet away.

A drifter dressed in filthy jeans and a long flannel shirt started to move forward. The man had a pinched, mean face and a two-day growth of beard. He had been loitering outside the rest rooms of the gas station, near the candy machines. He didn't look like a wino, exactly, more like a dirtbag flimflam man, a panhandler, a punk.

Probably going to check for coins in the pay phones. Or maybe pull a robbery.

In midstride, Gadgets halted and pointed at the man.

"Touch that phone, and I'll kill you." His voice cut like a knife.

"Hey, man, I was..."

"You say another word, creep, and I'll kill you."

The creep froze, unsure of what to do. Then, determination apparently overcame good sense—or fear—and he gazed balefully at the man in tan.

"Fuck you, man!" The words came out in a malevolent snarl. "I can touch anything I fucking want to touch." He made a grab for the dangling receiver with one hand, and poked in the coin return with the grubby index finger of the other.

A sharp metallic click cut through the muted roar of the midmorning traffic on the freeway. He turned around and found himself face to face with the muzzle of Gadgets's .45.

"I'm not kidding, creep. Split!" Gadgets's voice was low and deadly.

Moments later, the Able Team man was back on the telephone. The creep had vanished. In his place was the lingering odor of old B.O. and, Gadgets suspected, new urine.

"What was that all about?" demanded Brognola.

"Nothing. Just a minor matter of ridding the neighborhood of undesirables, Chief."

"Oh. Did you check the briefcase?"

"Yes."

"Well? Is it there? The Lambda report?"

"Affirmative. There's a whole file on it. At least, that's the name on the file tab."

Gadgets heard a long sigh of relief from the other end of the line. Then Brognola spoke, his voice tired but crisp.

"Get back here, code three. And don't let that file out of your sight. If you need to take a leak, take that file to the can with you. Shower with it. Better yet, don't shower at all. Catch the first plane here. We'll meet this evening in the conference room."

"What about—"

Brognola cut him off. "I'll notify the others." Then he stopped suddenly, as if he remembered something. "Come to think of it..." He hesitated.

"Yes, Chief?"

"Blancanales is out there in L.A. I'm going to have him meet up with you." He evidently thought for a few more moments. "Yes," he affirmed, "that's how we'll play it."

"The Politician's gonna hook up with me?"

"Yes." Brognola's voice was definitive. "Stand by where you are. I'll raise Blancanales and get him to you, code three, as Lyons would put it. Then the two of you can get to the airport and get back here."

"Ten-four, Chief."

Almost as an afterthought, Brognola added, "You see any problems with going back to the airport? After your little, er, contribution earlier?"

Gadgets grinned into the telephone. "Negative, Chief. No sweat for the chameleon."

"I didn't think so. Put on a different pair of glasses or spike up your hair or something. That's what they call it these days, isn't it? When they wear their hair in points?"

"Yes, Chief. Not 'spike up,' just 'spike.'" Gadgets hesitated. "Uh, Chief, pardon me for asking, but how are you going to handle this with Lyons?"

A second sigh came over the line. It sounded tired and infinitely sad. Any doubts Gadgets might have entertained about whether Brognola cared about the human side of things were instantly dispelled by the emotion in that sigh.

"Yeah, I guess I didn't want to dwell on that one. So I'm on the phone talking about spiked hair, Jesus." He sighed again. "I don't know, but I will. I'll handle that, too."

He paused, then repeated, almost to himself, "Sweet Jesus, I'll handle that one, too." Then, abruptly, his voice became crisp and controlled again. "Stand by that pay phone and wait for your buddy."

"Don't you need the address?"

"No. While we've been talking, the Bear has gotten all that for me. And, incidentally, checked the line."

"Oh," said Gadgets. "I should have known."

"Yes. Stony Man out."

6

The telephone call had come through to the motel room where Rosario "the Politician" Blancanales was staying. Although he had not been under orders to stand by for such a call, Blancanales had in fact been in his room when the telephone rang. Within two or three minutes, he was getting into his rented car, which was parked right outside his room.

A thrill of anticipation swelled in his body. It was the familiar feeling of orders received, dangers to be faced. It never ceased to affect him that way.

In truth, despite his devotion to the cause, he knew that this thrill of impending battle was one of the main things that kept him in the business.

To put it bluntly, he liked it.

When he left the motel, Blancanales was carrying only the clothes on his back, a .45 Colt Government Model pistol on his hip and a single briefcase in his hand. Although he knew he would not be returning to the room, he did not bother to stop at the counter to check out.

The room would be paid for later. Brognola would take care of that.

Nothing remained there to identify the man who had occupied it except anonymous clothes and toiletries. Anybody who checked the register would learn that the occupant had been a Señor Rolando Gonzalez of R.G. Enterprises in San Diego. The clerk might recall Mr. Gonzalez as a muscular Latin of medium height, well dressed, who spoke very little English.

Like Gadgets, the Politician was no neophyte when it came to looking inconspicuous.

And, when the supposed representative of the fictitious R.G. Enterprises appeared later than evening to pay the rent on the room, in cash, he would first collect those items of clothing and toiletries. He would also let slip to the desk clerk that Mr. Gonzalez's mother in Mexico City had suddenly been taken ill; hence, his abrupt departure.

The clerk wouldn't ask any questions.

He would have no reason to doubt what he had learned. More important, he wouldn't remember much, and what he did remember would be subconsciously influenced by what he had been told.

From the motel, it had taken Blancanales twenty-five frustrating minutes to cover the distance to the off ramp Gadgets had taken. The traffic, though not heavy, had been unpredictable—freeway speeds one minute, and the next a virtual standstill caused by no better reason than rubberneckers gawking at steam from an overheated car on the road's shoulder.

Blancanales rolled the rented Datsun through the stop sign at the foot of the ramp and turned right on the surface street.

For once, he thought, things had gone the way they were supposed to. It had been one of those rare instances when everything went like clockwork, even though "everything" was only the relatively simple process of Brognola making contact and Blancanales reacting.

It usually doesn't work that way, he thought. Maybe this makes up for one of the times when it ought to go well, but it actually turns to shit.

"Drop everything. We've got something hot." Brognola's voice had boomed, all business and none of the usual geniality, into his ear.

"Roger, Chief."

"Clear out of the room, and get to this location."

"Directions?"

Brognola had given them. Meet Gadgets there, he had said. Find him and nurse-maid the man and his briefcase back to HQ, ASAP.

"Roger, Chief," Blancanales had said a second time.

"Any questions?"

"Just one."

"Shoot."

"What zone?"

Brognola hesitated only an instant. "Red. Now get moving. Stony Man out."

Rosario Blancanales, aka the Politician, the soldier-turned-counterterrorist, had needed no further explanation. The orders were clear, the essential points covered. Questions like "what's up," "why," and "what's in the briefcase" were for amateurs.

Blancanales was no amateur.

Apart from the who, what and where—the why being regarded by both men as largely irrelevant—the rest of what the Politician needed to know was contained in the specification that this was a red-zone matter.

In the jargon of its clandestine activities, the world of Stony Man Farm—its operational world, at least—was divided into four zones. The main distinguishing factors were, primarily, the degree of danger and, secondarily, the agent's proximity to the target of his mission.

The range went from target zone at the highest, to red, yellow and finally white.

Red zone was the second to the highest stage of awareness, a state of full alert. The designation was applied, albeit with some flexibility, to two situations. The first occurred when the team was closing in on the enemy, but the battle had not yet been joined.

The second usage of the term came about whenever they were in some especially dangerous aspect of the mission. It might be that the particular phase was still relatively far removed from the ultimate target. Still, if the risk of hostile contact was quite high, it got a red zone classification, regardless of how early it was in the mission.

It was this second meaning that both men gave to the term "red zone" as Brognola had used it in his brief conversation with Blancanales.

This was especially so since—from the Politician's viewpoint, at least—no mission had yet been assigned. To use the red-zone designation was a short way of telling him "extreme danger, watch your ass, the threat could come from anywhere." That message, along with the "where" and the "what," told the Politician everything he needed to know.

Red.

Expect hostile contact. And expect to have to shoot your way out of it.

In the manner of military and police specialists, or for that matter, anybody who works in a profession with unique jargon or terminology, the terms had made their way into the ordinary conversation of Blancanales, Gadgets and Carl Lyons.

The terms became broadened, used in a more general sense, to describe any situation.

For instance, if one of them had fallen into a snake pit, or maybe had very nearly gotten engaged or—perish the thought—married, or faced some unspeakable danger, real or imagined, he might have commented, "Yeah, for a moment there, it was real close."

"Pretty hairy, huh?"

"Yep. It was red zone all the way."

The only zone higher than red was target, which meant the mission was coming to a head. Usually, for Able Team, at least, that meant they were either in a firefight or going into one momentarily. By contrast, yellow and white signified stages of correspondingly less danger.

In military terms, yellow zone was roughly comparable to fifty-percent alert. Red would be full alert. The lowest designation, white, was rarely used.

Carl Lyons, making a disgusted commentary on the standards of cops his old alma mater, LAPD, was recruiting these days, once offered a sarcastic description of white zone.

"If I were still with the PD, white zone would be making sure your trainee's Seeing Eye dog wasn't on drugs."

Gadgets Schwarz had agreed. "In white zone, all you have to worry about is drunk drivers and the flu."

"I can think of a couple of other things," Lyons had muttered.

"Such as?"

"Attorneys, rattlesnakes and sharks."

"I like how you lump those together, Ironman."

Lyons went on, unabated. "Liberal judges. Attorneys. The Supreme Court. And all the others who intentionally or unintentionally are bringing down the system from within."

Gadgets whistled. "Jesus, Ironman. What gives with the heavy philosophical shit all of a sudden? Flashback to a bad acid trip or something?"

And, to his credit, Lyons had grinned a little sheepishly. "Sorry, guys. Flashback to something, I guess. Not an acid trip, though. This fucking job—hell, this fucking *life* gives me enough weird trips that drugs are the last thing I need."

"Welcome back, Ironman." Gadgets had smiled.

"But speaking of the dangers of white zone," Lyons continued, "I've got a couple more."

"Oh, yeah? This isn't going to be like your last examples, is it, oh harbinger of gloom?"

"Nope. Nothing like that. It's cheap booze and ugly women."

At this point, Blancanales, who had been watching, interceded. "That's easy to avoid. Just don't buy cheap booze, and don't go to bed with ugly women."

Lyons winked. "I've never gone to bed with an ugly woman," he quipped. "But I've woken up with a few."

"I know the feeling," Blancanales said, nodding and flashing his easy politician's grin. "A 'closing-time ten.' I've met one or two in my time."

"That's the cheap booze," pointed out Gadgets. "Stay away from it, and you won't be waking up with beasts. See? The booze is the root of all your problems."

"Good point."

The son of illegal immigrants who had crossed into the U.S. from Mexico before he was born, Blancanales had grown up in the streets of Southern California. Specifically, he had lived in East Los Angeles and in San Ysidro, the latter a border town between San Diego on the U.S. side and Tijuana on the Mexican side.

His parents were hardworking, decent folks, determined to make it in America. At eighteen, the Politician had been a lean, athletic young man. He had lived on the streets, and had learned their ways. He carried a scar or two from encounters with members of street gangs who didn't like his looks, or his presence on their turf, or who had some other imaginary grudge against him.

He had also, if the truth be known, given out better than he had gotten in the scar department.

But beneath it all, the young Blancanales had grown up possessed of an easy, charming smile and his father's profound sense of responsibility. It was a sort of gratitude, actually, for the chance to live in a country where opportunity existed for anybody who would work for it.

It hadn't taken him long to figure it out.

The young man had looked around at those who were successful, and those who weren't. He had seen the business people, the elected officials, the workers, and the takers. He had seen the powerful and the weak, the righteous and the corrupt.

And through it all, he had developed a rugged sense of honesty and, if possible, an even deeper appreciation of the American dream than his father had possessed.

At eighteen, he joined the army. For him, that meant basic training, followed by Airborne School. In later years, he completed a number of specialized schools, most of them sponsored officially or unofficially by Uncle Sam, including one on jungle warfare.

If you're gonna do it at all, do it all, he thought.

In Vietnam he had slogged through jungle mud while students at state universities flattened fences and burned banks. He was wounded and decorated. As a soldier he had done whatever was necessary, sometimes reckless, sometimes cautious, always professional.

Also in Vietnam, he had met the man who would ultimately recruit him for Stony Man Farm. That meeting had changed his life and, indirectly, changed—or ended—the lives of a lot of people on the other side, the bad guys, terrorists and predators.

Although he killed when he had to, Blancanales was not like that.

As a soldier, he had been one of the ones the others had looked up to. And he had been that way due in large part to his sense of fairness and his quiet, fatalistic calm in the face of danger.

Quiet and fatalistic, that is, until circumstances required him to become a raging, hard-hitting, fast-moving warrior.

Anybody who had served in combat situations knew the type. Officers, even little college-boy second looies, recognized it. The smart ones used it to the advantage of the whole platoon.

And the other enlisted men, especially the scared nineteen-year-olds trying to do what was right a million miles away from home and family, saw it and looked up to it. They silently watched and drew courage from Blancanales's lack of fear. It was as if his quiet bravery was in a positive sense contagious, something that could be shared without being used up.

When he was alone in combat, or nearly alone, Blancanales had the same silent, strong courage.

One time—this was in another jungle, not Nam, but one much closer to home—he had been called upon to show it.

He had been part of a small advisory and intelligence mission, top secret. It was at a time when the White House angrily denied having "any active personnel in Central America." The Russians had been equally emphatic, and more vocal in their denial of having advisers in that part of the world. But despite what the records said, including the files on the men involved, there was a handful of scattered personnel—from both nations—very active in the countries south of Mexico.

The Politician had been one of them.

That night, Blancanales and his partner were crouched in the heavy, damp jungle. They were waiting for night to fall, expecting a rendezvous between Communist advisers and local guerrilla fighters. They had learned of the meeting, and their mission was to confirm or deny, to verify if it in fact took place.

It happened about four hours after nightfall.

The two Black Berets, both jungle warfare specialists, had been concealed in the thick undergrowth, waiting and watching.

The meeting in fact occurred, or "went down," in the jargon of the trade. The two U.S. soldiers crouched and watched as Soviet advisers met with local guerrillas. And, in the midst of it, Blancanales felt something.

It began as more of a presence than anything else. His ears and other senses, all fine-tuned, detected it first. The faintest rustle, more of a shifting, actually, of leaves. Then he felt it.

It began as a tickle. It felt like a spiderweb or a feather that one wipes away from one's skin. It grew until it covered his whole body and that of his companion, a man everybody called J. W. Fish, the J.W. reportedly standing simply for Jungle Warfare.

Insects!

A sudden, slight hiss, the catching of breath close by, told him that his fellow soldier had felt the same thing. Then Blancanales heard the faintest whisper, as Fish breathed two words.

"Army ants!"

Visions of thousands of the little creatures, their tiny dry legs and feet picking their way over the pores of his flesh, swarmed into Blancanales's mind. It was all he could do not to scream, to leap up, to start the slapstick comedy routine of swatting and brushing and stripping off the clothes.

But to do so would alert the enemy. The mission would be blown, and certain torture and death would result. The press would have a field day, and the liberal U.S. Congress would further hamstring defense efforts.

It was impossible to see in the pitch-blackness. But what they couldn't detect by the sense of sight was more than offset by the sense of touch, as every nerve ending in their skin was activated by the tiny creatures.

The Politician thought he would go mad.

The dry tickling grew and spread until it covered his body. The ants were everywhere, over his clothing, under his clothing, on his arms, his face, his neck, his chest, back, legs, groin....

Desperately, Blancanales tried to remember what he had learned in Jungle Warfare School.

They had talked about ants, along with a million other insects. And, under the numbing stress of the school, he had listened only to part of it, figuring that the best way was to simply avoid the goddamn things.

What had the instructors said?

There were two kinds of so-called army ants, he recalled. One type lived in the western hemisphere, including Central America. The other, actually called driver ants, lived in Africa.

One kind didn't eat animals or people, despite stories and legends to the contrary. This variety ate only other arthropods. The second kind did eat people, and had sharp, scissorslike mandibles or jaws that sliced through flesh quite nicely.

Which was which?

Was it the western hemisphere guys who were the friendlies, or was it the African types? At every moment, Blancanales could imagine the onslaught of a thousand tiny razors slicing into his flesh.

He longed to swear under his breath, to curse, but no oath or epithet seemed strong enough. Not even the boot camp standby, "rat shit, cat shit, dirty old twat—sixty-nine assholes tied in a knot."

Every nerve in his body was stretched to the breaking point. Slowly, with infinite care, Blancanales rose and backed off a few yards. J.W. did likewise.

Blancanales sensed his comrade's presence in the pitch-darkness, mainly by instinct. Putting his mouth close to J.W.'s ear, he breathed, "They biting you?"

"No. You?"

"No. Must be the good brand."

"Yeah."

"You know what, though, J.W.?"

"What, Blanc?"

"It still sucks."

"If I get out of this, I swear I'll never eat a chocolate-covered ant again."

"I never ate any in the first place."

Wordlessly, Blancanales set down his M-16 on the jungle floor. Then, with exquisite slowness to prevent the slightest click, snap or other sound, he began to strip. Without being told, and without seeing it, for that matter, Fish did likewise.

For the next eternity—actually about twenty minutes—the two soldiers performed their soundless, slow-motion striptease. And all the while, only yards away, heavily armed Soviet military advisers and Central American guerrillas plotted their takeovers, trying to topple yet another domino in the march to the U.S.

Clothing gone, each man lightly brushed again and again the surfaces of their bodies. Next they turned and brushed each other's backs. Then, equally painstakingly, they brushed out their jungle clothing, and slowly redressed.

A half hour or so later, they were back in position—though a position a few yards away from the path of the ants—doing the job Uncle Sam paid them to do.

Months later, Blancanales looked it up. Sure enough, the western hemisphere's army ants were the friendly kind—at least to man—while the African breed were the ones with the sharp nippers and equally sharp appetites.

Today, in his late thirties, Blancanales was heavier than he had been as a young man.

He was stocky and strong, with a dense, well-defined musculature and a deceptive quickness despite his solid physique. His hair was a startling combination of jet-black and streaks of gray, and his face was deeply lined. Yet somehow he maintained an almost youthful appearance, and a personal energy that shone through like a light whenever he flashed his easy politician's grin.

There was another side to him, however, apart from his dedication to constitution and country. And, in fact, this other side in many ways masked the strength of his personal beliefs, and his willingness to die for them.

The other side was what most people saw.

It was a cheerfulness, a vitality and good humor that marked his approach to life. He had a strong, aquiline nose, and expressive dark brown eyes. The features of his face added up to uniquely Latin good looks, and an unquenchable love of life.

"Joie de vivre," as a very special woman had once described it.

"What? *¿Qué dices?*" he had responded, his voice a tender whisper.

"Joie de vivre," she had repeated. She had been lying on top of him, straddling him, in the bed of her Georgetown apartment. She'd had gentle, sensitive features, and the light had danced in her long, honey-colored hair. She was an instructor in English literature at a prestigious liberal-arts college, and she was the most refined lover Blancanales had ever been with.

"What does it mean?"

She had emitted a gentle sigh, and looked down at him, supporting herself with her hands by his shoulders. "Something akin to a 'love of life.' Like a joy of being alive. A zest."

He had looked up into her eyes and smiled.

"Oh, God," she said in a tone of helpless submission.

"What is it?"

"The smile. It's the smile. It's the contrast, your face 'before and after.' It's the...oh, hell, I don't know what it is."

He regarded her in bemused silence.

"Your smile," she began again. "It's not one smile, it's a thousand smiles. It's what keeps those brown eyes of yours from being insufferably soulful."

"Why 'insufferable'? What's wrong with soulful?" he asked in mock seriousness.

"Nothing's *wrong* with it," she responded. "It's just that this—your face, that is—has so much more character. It's innocent and wicked at the same time. It's...you look like an altar boy with a delicious, naughty little secret."

At this he smiled. "In case you haven't guessed, *mi guapa*, I'm no altar boy."

"Do you have a naughty little secret, then?" she teased him, her voice gently taunting.

Again, the smile. "Secrets too numerous to mention," he responded.

Again, the smile was hiding the man. If you only knew, he thought, of the secrets I have. Secret memories of life, and death, and courage, and fear; secret visions of freedoms, and of chains, and of man's eternal struggle to achieve one and avoid the other.

But of course she couldn't know, just as nobody could know who hadn't seen the same kinds of things, which was perhaps part of the special bond that all true warriors share.

Today, though, he wasn't thinking of this woman, or of secrets, or anything other than to get to Gadgets as fast as he could. Then the two of them could get to high ground, so to speak, and once they were sure no immediate hostile aggression awaited them, make their way to Stony Man Farm as Brognola directed.

The car radio was on as he drove. Emergency news bulletins told him of the terrorist attack at the airport. And although Brognola had not advised him of it, the Politician knew the coincidence was too great.

Blancanales pulled the car into the parking lot of a Denny's restaurant before he saw Gadgets's rented sedan near the pay phone across the street. But he didn't see Gadgets.

A pang of concern struck him. His eyes scanned first the car, then the area around it—the gas station, the metal dumpster, the cars parked nearby—looking for any sign of his partner.

Nothing.

Guiding the car with his left hand on the wheel, the Politician reached easily to his right hip with the other hand. Moments later, his right hand was in his lap, forearm across his thigh.

The hand now held a .45 pistol. It was identical in all respects to the one Gadgets carried, thanks to the efforts of Stony Man's weaponsmith, John "Cowboy" Kissinger. Blancanales held the weapon casually, most of it concealed between his thighs. Then he drove the car across the street and cruised into the lot.

Pretending not to show any interest in the empty sedan, he made a slow sweep past the gas pumps, then on around the building.

Moments later, he emerged from behind the building.

This time, the Politician was on foot, wearing a hip-length brown leather coat. His hands were in the side pockets of the coat, and his shoulders were hunched as if against a cold wind.

He checked the car.

Nothing. It was locked, and had the clean, anonymous look common to rental cars.

Something moved, off to the side, barely in his peripheral vision. Blancanales crouched and turned in a single, swift movement, his right hand starting to come out of his jacket.

He found himself staring into his partner's face.

"*Hola*, Homes," said Gadgets. "Did I startle you?" His features moved into a smile, but he clearly wasn't in a smiling mood.

"*Hola*. What're you up to, amigo?"

"Waiting for you, I gather."

"Well, I'm here." Blancanales's voice was grim. "What's going on?"

Gadgets give him a brief sketch of what had happened. As the Politician listened, his expressive face became a mixture of anger and loss. "Ay, *Dios*," he muttered at last. "She's dead? No doubt about it?"

Gadgets nodded glumly.

The Politician thought for a moment. "Say, amigo. Any sign of anybody following you?"

"The chief asked that, too. I didn't pay too much attention, but I'd say not. In fact, I'm sure not."

"Why are you so sure?"

"Look. I just was trying to get out of there, Homes," Gadgets said, his voice a little sharp. "But I didn't see anybody obviously following me. Besides, who would there be? I just blew away the two guys who did it."

"Unless..."

"Unless what? Are you suggesting there might have been somebody else there? An accomplice?"

"*Sí*, amigo. There had to be, the way I see it."

"What do you mean?"

"Look at it this way. That briefcase—or the Lambda report inside it—was of immense importance to El Jefe, Brognola. Am I right?"

"Yes."

"So it seems likely that the killers were after it. And after Julie because she had it."

"And maybe because she had other information not in the file," agreed Gadgets.

"Possibly. But my point is, you said the two killers were starting to run when you nailed them."

"So?"

"So, if we assume the briefcase was what they were really after, there must have been somebody else there who was going to get it after the shooting."

"A third man?" speculated Gadgets, intrigued.

"*Sí*, amigo. Did you see anything like that?"

Gadgets thought back. "No," he finally said. "Just the ordinary crowd. Businessmen, families, nothing that really sticks out."

"Okay. That's something, anyway." Blancanales relaxed slightly, though he had no intention of altering his red zone behavior. "At least we seem to be in the clear for the time being, anyway."

Gadgets nodded.

At precisely that moment, the blast of a shotgun split the gray, midwinter air.

7

"Look out!"

"Shit!"

The side window of Gadgets's car exploded into a thousand chunks and chips of glass. Simultaneously came the splintery crash of the impact mingled with a distinctly metallic clank as some of the bullet-size pellets of buckshot hit metal instead of glass.

Blancanales's shouted warning wasn't necessary. Nor, for that matter, was Gadgets's one-word rejoinder.

Even as he yelled his own comment, Gadgets was already looking out. He did this by executing a combination back flip and high jump over the hood of his rented car. It was an awkward maneuver, but what it lacked in grace it made up for in enthusiasm.

Glass and metal fragments flew again as a second shotgun blast struck the sedan's front fender, precisely where Gadgets had been standing.

He landed heavily on his knees on the far side of the car. Wrenching the .45 from his belt, Gadgets noticed the front wheel was almost immediately before him.

He moved sideways a few inches so it would, in fact, be between him and the enemy.

Steel-belted radials, he knew, would deflect buckshot quite nicely.

The Politician moved equally fast.

Digging in like a sprinter or a quarter horse, he surged to the left, away from Gadgets and the rented car. A few feet in front of him stood the dilapidated body of a truck. Blancanales launched himself into a headfirst dive like a racing swimmer entering the pool in the hundred-meter freestyle. He skidded on his stomach along the dirty pavement, but it was better than acting as a backstop to the third blast from the attacker's shotgun.

Pistol now in hand, Blancanales rolled to his feet and peered over the hood of the old truck.

Both men saw their attackers bearing down on them.

The enemy were in two vehicles, one after the other. Both headed straight for Gadgets's rental car, which he now crouched behind, gun in hand.

The first was a black Lincoln Continental. It swayed on its soft suspension as it swerved, motor roaring and tires yelping, into the entrance of the gas station. A shower of sparks flew as the undercarriage crashed against the gutter.

Behind it was a van, driven by a man in Dodger blue. It swerved dangerously, almost going out of control, as it attempted to follow the black car.

Tires screeched as the Lincoln bore down on them. Then both men saw a man's torso above the roof of the car—a legless man riding on top of the massive vehicle, getting ready to fire his next shot!

"What the—!"

Gadgets's amazed cry was cut short by another shotgun blast. A vivid orange flame came from the weapon held by the man atop the charging Lincoln Continental.

With a metallic crash, the buckshot hit Gadgets's sedan in the rear quarter-panel.

Christ, he thought, buckshot is some scary shit indeed!

The legless man held a cutoff pump shotgun. Through the windows of the Continental, Gadgets and Blancanales could make out the shapes of more men inside the massive car. They could also see the narrow, long objects held by the men.

And somehow, neither Gadgets nor the Politician thought those men were just holding umbrellas.

Tires screeched on the gravelly pavement as the car accelerated, engine roaring. It resembled some terrifying surrealistic, anachronistic knight riding a massive black steed, wielding a shotgun instead of a battle-ax or sword or lance.

For just an instant, Gadgets froze as his mind tried to digest what his eyes were telling it.

Then the Lincoln fishtailed in its charge toward them, and they saw that the man wasn't legless at all. Instead, he was a perfectly ordinary man standing inside the car, with his body emerging through the sunroof, and his feet, probably, planted on the passenger's seat and center console respectively.

A perfectly ordinary man in the form of a killer getting ready to fire yet another blast from the shotgun, that is.

The realization galvanized Gadgets and Blancanales into action at last.

Boom! Boom! Boom! Boom!

Gadgets fired four times from the .45 as the Lincoln bore down on him. He fired by instinct, the thinking part of his mind for once shut down by the red-zone, save-your-life reflexes. Then he didn't have time to shoot anymore, and the Lincoln was smashing into his car.

His cover.

As he fired, Gadgets had no conscious idea where he was placing his shots, other than at that big fucking car coming toward him with the guy and the shotgun.

His first shot hit the windshield dead center. The thick safety glass, slanting upward away from him, deflected the massive soft-tipped .45 slug off into the distance. The bullet made the high-pitched banshee's wail of a ricochet after its impact.

Not that Gadgets was consciously aware of any of this.

If he had been aware, though, he would have realized that the first shot represented a rare moment of indecision for him. Faced with the choice of shooting at the gunman, who was more to the passenger side of the car as he stuck through the sunroof, or the driver, he had done neither. The first slug had split the difference, hitting left—from Gadgets's perspective—of

Ghost Train 89

the driver but right of the gunman sticking out of the roof.

And missing both.

The second round was like the first, only more to the passenger side or to the left. It, too, ricocheted off the windshield, glancing upward.

Directly into the belly of the gunman out the sunroof, a paralyzing and fatal hit actually made worse because it was a ricochet instead of a straight-on hit.

The impact on the heavy safety glass deformed the silver-tip .45 slug into an irregular-shaped blob about three-quarters of an inch across.

The laws of physics meant the bullet lost a little velocity—and hence a few foot-pounds of energy—from the change in direction. It still had plenty of "punch" to it, though. Moreover, the impact off the windshield caused the slug to "mushroom," or spread out to present a larger surface area.

In the horrifying science of wound ballistics, this mushrooming effect is exactly what is sought by soft-point, hollow-point, or silver-tip types of slugs. The bigger the surface area of the projectile, generally speaking, the more its energy is transferred to, and absorbed by, the target.

When the target is human flesh, the result is greater destruction of tissue and a higher mortality rate.

Here, the enlarged missile from Gadgets's second shot smacked into the soft flesh of the killer's abdomen just above the navel and below the ribs. The impact was roughly equivalent to being hit with a seventy- or eighty-caliber bullet, if such a thing existed.

The shotgun went flying as dying nerve reflexes made the killer double up around the numbing pain in his midsection.

Rounds three and four went dead center into the driver.

The first two shots, though ricochets, had smashed and starred the windshield into a spiderweb network of a million cracks. These radiated outward in all directions from each impact.

Thus weakened, the windshield lacked the strength to deflect the last two shots.

The driver took them both, one in the upper chest and the other a couple of inches directly above the first, in the neck.

Ironically, both shots were, in a sense, wasted.

Off to one side, from his position behind the old truck, Blancanales had begun firing an instant before Gadgets had. One round was low, striking the driver's door and failing to penetrate.

The second round hit the window on the rear door.

It went through the glass nicely and took out another gunman in the back seat. The deformed slug hit him in the side of the head, just above the left ear. The impact both broke his neck and stirred his brains in a single, terrible display of physics and wound ballistics.

The third round went through the window of the driver's door. Like the one before it, it hit the man on the side of his cranium. The results were as deadly.

Ghost Train

Lights out.

Permanently, and a split instant before Gadgets's two slugs tore in from the front.

The driver's body spasmed into rigidity as the shattered brain and nerves sent conflicting, overloaded signals to the muscles. One result of this was that the foot jammed the accelerator to the floor.

The Continental leaped forward, straight at Gadgets.

It didn't take a rocket scientist to realize that the rental sedan—calling it even a midsize car stretched credibility—would not withstand the impact from the massive Lincoln. Again, acting on instinct, the counterterrorist reacted.

Not to the left. Not to the right. No time for either of those.

Straight up was the only option.

He rose from his crouch with a powerful thrust of his legs. In a sense, it was like a standing high jump, a jump straight upward, tucking the legs up, knees to chest. All he had to do to avoid the immediate danger was clear the front fender and hood.

He made it easily, thanks to the fear that added strength and considerable vigor to his leap.

The Continental struck the sedan with a metal-rending crash. The lighter vehicle was knocked sideways, directly over the spot where Gadgets had been. The Able Team commando ended up on the hood, not of his own car, but of the Lincoln. He struck there roughly on all fours, facing into the shattered windshield, the .45 still clenched in his fist.

For the briefest instant, he caught a terrible glimpse of the ruined face of the dead driver. Then the windshield of the onrushing Lincoln hit him, and he bounced up and over the roof.

"Huumph!"

The impact drove the air from Gadgets's lungs in a painful grunt. Shock and pain shot through him as his left shoulder hit the Lincoln's windshield right where it joined the metal roof. The blow flipped him violently up and onto the vehicle's roof. He struck partly on top of the dead gunman whose body still hung half in and half out of the sunroof. Then the Lincoln had gone under him, and he was bouncing down behind it, off the deck of the trunk and onto the pavement.

Dazed, bleeding from his mouth and from a gash in the skin over his cheekbone, both incurred when he hit the windshield of the Lincoln, Gadgets rolled to his knees and tried to rise.

From behind the truck, the horrified Blancanales saw his partner's slow struggle to get to his feet.

He also saw the second vehicle, the van driven by the man in blue.

Earlier, the van had skidded wide to one side as the Continental charged toward Gadgets's car. Now, however, with a screech of tires, it started to swing back around toward the dazed commando.

It seemed to Blancanales that the scene unfolded in slow motion, a dreadful frame-by-frame advance of a movie film.

It was a scene where the last frame would show his partner being shot and run over by the van, if he didn't do something about it.

Frame. The Politician leaned across the hood of the old truck. The length of his right arm rested along the rusty metal surface, providing a stable bench rest from which to shoot.

Frame. Gravel streaming from the rear tires, the van continued to swing toward Gadgets.

Frame. Blancanales leaned into the truck body, and his left hand found the right one, the gun hand, for added stability. He could see the man in bright blue cranking the wheel hard around. Smoke rose from the squealing rear tires.

Frame. With agonizing slowness, Gadgets started to turn toward the threat.

Blancanales could see it would be too little, too late.

Frame. The van was broadside to the Politician, the driver's window a flat surface facing him. He could see the shiny metallic blue of the driver's clothing.

Frame. Boom!

The .45 jumped in his hand. An empty brass shell casing clinked on the pavement.

A neat hole appeared in the driver's side window of the van. A spiderweb of cracks radiated outward in all directions from it.

Boom! Boom! Boom!

More holes in the window, more cracks, and the man in Dodger blue died instantly as all four shots, for once, were perfectly on target.

Driverless, the van couldn't maintain its tight, screeching circle toward Gadgets. Instead, it lurched off on a tangent and struck the building of the service station, where it exploded in a fiery petrochemical ball of orange flame and black smoke.

Blancanales saw his still-dazed companion, now on his feet, turn slowly toward the fireball.

"Gadgets!" he shouted urgently. "Over here!

Even as he was speaking, the Politician was aware that more hostiles were likely present. There could be somebody else in the van; certainly there was at least one more man in the Lincoln.

One-handed, he dropped the clip from his .45, then inserted a new one and clapped it into place with the palm of his left hand. He did it by feel, never taking his eyes off the panorama before him—the ruined Lincoln crushed against the ruined rental sedan; his partner and friend making his unsteady way back toward him; and beyond them, the brightly burning van.

"Hurry, Gadgets!" he called urgently.

His friend appeared to shake his head, as if trying to shed the effects of some opiate. Then his eyes focused, and Gadgets began to jog toward him.

"Coming, Homes," he said, a ragged grin cutting across his tired features.

Suddenly, he stopped.

"What's the matter?" demanded the Politician urgently. In the distance, a siren wailed. "We've gotta haul ass, man!"

"Not without the briefcase, we don't."

Blancanales nodded. "*Bueno pues*. Get it and let's make ourselves the hell scarce around here." With a final look at the Continental—no action there, the gunman was either knocked out or lying low—Blancanales emerged from his cover.

Moments later, the two men and their precious cargo were in the Politician's car. As the wail of the sirens grew louder, Blancanales inserted the ignition key and started the engine. For several heart-stopping seconds, it ground and turned over without catching. Finally, it started, and they lurched back onto the surface.

A right and a left put them on the on ramp, heading back up onto the freeway.

With a faint, sardonic smile, Blancanales turned to his still-shaken friend. "As I was saying, at least we're in the clear for the time being. Right, amigo?"

Gadgets started to shake his head in wonderment, then stopped abruptly as the motion torqued his painful shoulder. Still, he managed a grin in return.

"Right on, Homes," he said sighing. "Right on."

8

The conference room at Stony Man Farm was located on the ground floor of the main building.

Home base for Able Team—and a number of other similar tactical groups just as secret as Able—the Farm lay in the Blue Ridge Mountains of Virginia. It got its name from Stony Man Mountain, which at some four thousand feet above sea level was one of the highest peaks in the area.

In actual size, the Farm consisted of a quarter section, or 160 acres, of land.

The acreage was almost but not quite rectangular. Strictly speaking, it could be described as a tall trapezoid, though with not much difference in length between the two bases—or between the top and the bottom, depending on how technical the description. It was about eighty miles as the crow—or a helicopter—flies from Washington, D.C.

The area was thickly wooded, a dense forest of pine, fir and a variety of hardwoods. An airstrip had been cleared in the northwest corner; the main buildings lay in the approximate center of the land.

Remote, private and equipped with the latest in computer technology—the main computers were located in a separate structure, with special environmental controls to dissipate the heat the huge machines generated—Stony Man Farm was the permanent headquarters for Hal Brognola and Aaron Kurtzman, along with a staff of trusted assistants.

It was also the site of a very grim meeting called for 10:00 a.m. the morning following the LAX massacre.

Brognola had originally instructed Gadgets and Blancanales to report to Stony Man Farm ASAP. To back up his order, he had scheduled a meeting for that same night, 10:00 p.m. Eastern Standard Time.

He had then proceeded to locate Lyons—which involved the unpleasant task of breaking the devastating news about Julie—and had told him the same thing.

By midafternoon, however, Brognola had realized that a meeting that evening would be premature, and moreover, that such an accelerated schedule was probably not necessary. Accordingly, he had rescheduled it for the following morning.

Breaking the news about Julie's death to Lyons had been a tough one for the Stony Man chief. Now, as he reflected on it, Brognola was still not sure of its effect on his ace commando.

At first the Ironman had seemed curiously unaffected by the incident.

"Are you sure, Chief?" His voice had been deadly calm, as he asked a question similar to that asked by Brognola himself when Gadgets made his report.

"I'm sure, Carl."

"I see."

"I'm sorry, Carl."

"Yeah. Thanks." Then, after a moment's pause, he went on. "Are there any details?"

"Some." Brognola had proceeded to supply the sketchy facts in his possession. Lyons had listened, and made a comment or clarifying question at a couple of points. Still, he'd seemed so remote that for the briefest moment Brognola wondered if he had been wrong about the depth of their feelings for each other.

Then he had dismissed that thought.

He could not be wrong about that part. Lyons had indeed been in love with Julie, despite the almost eerie lack of emotion he'd shown when Brognola broke the news to him. No, he's just being stoic, the Stony Man chief concluded at last.

Then an even more troubling thought hit him. Was this going to be the straw—hell, the ton of bricks—that broke the Ironman's back? Was he going to flip out at last?

Two implications of that possibility disturbed him.

One was humane, or humanitarian. He felt a strong affection for Lyons, that special bond among fighting men and friends that transcended the subordinate/leader relationship. It would be a personal tragedy of incredible proportions—to Lyons, of course, but also to Brognola—if the Ironman cracked.

The second had tactical overtones.

If Lyons did crack up, how would he do it? Or, more precisely, how would he show it? Would he go berserk, becoming the avenging angel and cutting a swath of death and destruction among any enemy who he might believe had been involved in her death?

Or would he just quietly blow his brains out?

Brognola was a master tactician in the coldest, dirtiest war going, the war against terrorists. This required that he have the ability to be as ruthless and cold-blooded a bastard as the animals he fought against, given the right circumstances.

As one of his subordinates had put it, Brognola "had been there and back."

He did what it took to survive, and to hold off the terrorist enemy. And, in the arena where they fought, that kind of calculating ruthlessness was properly regarded as an asset, rather than a character flaw.

In fact, it had been Carl Lyons himself who once pointed that out. It had occurred following a briefing on a particularly sensitive operation, one that had been undertaken at the request of the President himself. And, in typical Lyons style, the Ironman had been "right out front with it"—despite the fact that the person he was addressing was a White House envoy.

The envoy, who Lyons had instantly determined was an ivory-tower silver-spooner with no "real world" experience, had made the comment that the scheme Brognola had proposed "seemed a little shocking."

Lyons had looked at the soft-handed Ivy Leaguer in amazement. "Shocking?" he repeated.

The envoy had nodded slightly.

"So, what's wrong with that?" demanded Lyons.

The others had regarded him with surprise. It wasn't really a subject that needed debating, of course, and certainly Brognola could defend himself, or endure the disapproval of this little Oval Office twit. But the man's high-handedness had been just too much for Lyons to take.

"Well," explained the envoy, "it does seem a little Machiavellian, if I may say so." He had that snooty college-professor way of speaking that seemed calculated to make his listeners feel like hicks.

"Machiavellian?" the Ironman had repeated, puzzled.

The envoy had given him a look that was gently, sadly patronizing. "Why, yes. Machiavelli, as you know—" here he'd made the slightest pause, just enough to imply that he clearly believed Lyons did *not* know "—was the Florentine statesman and political theorist whose teachings are popularly associated with the concept that 'the end justifies the means,' though of course he—"

"I know who the hell Machiavelli was," Lyons had interrupted curtly. "I didn't think he was some guy who played linebacker for the Raiders, for God's sake. I just want to know what your objection is to the chief's plan. *Of course* it's Machiavellian. So what?"

"Oh, well, it's more a matter of principle, actually. It just seems—"

"You got a better idea?"

"Ah, I suppose not. It's just that the, well, devious nature of the proposal...it is ingenious, I'll grant you that. It says something about Mr., ah, your chief, that he would—"

Lyons could contain himself no longer. "What the hell do you expect, for God's sake? You want fucking Tinkerbell leading our raids? Or negotiating with the Russians on arms limitations? Or—" and here he had recalled his cop days "—being your partner in breaking up bar fights between outlaw bikers?"

The man hadn't replied.

"Jesus," Lyons muttered, "this isn't the fucking tennis courts we're operating in, for God's sake."

It had looked as if he was going to say more, but Brognola had interceded to call off his dog. After he had waited until the Harvard nerd was suitably chastened, that is.

"That's all right, Carl. I'm sure these were just philosophical points, things better discussed another time." And the chief had gone on to smoothly continue the briefing, now with a much quieter envoy as his listener.

Today, however, it was precisely Brognola's ruthlessness that raised the second possible implication of the disturbing possibility that Lyons might crack under this latest stress.

It would be interesting, Brognola speculated, to see what kind of damage would be wrought on those Lyons believed were responsible. Take a skilled fighter, already brave and experienced, and allow him to go on a suicide mission fueled with an unquenchable vengeance....

The damage—to the enemy, whatever enemy it might be—would be high, possibly staggering.

Then Brognola the man overcame Brognola the strategist and he dismissed the thought. Lyons wouldn't crack. He wasn't like that.

The Ironman's apparent stoicism in the face of Julie's death was, Brognola felt certain, just that. He was being stoic. He would handle it his own way, privately coming to grips with it as much as he could and then putting the rest of it behind him to go on with business.

Maybe that was a good way to handle it, psychologically speaking, and maybe it wasn't. Brognola didn't know the answer to that. But it was certainly Lyons's way, and that was all there was to it.

In fact, Lyons did handle it in a manner that was somewhat as Brognola envisioned.

At another time in his life, the Ironman would have reacted differently. He would have gone through them all: first disbelief; then anger and self-pity—asking himself, "Why her? Why *me*?"; then despair and finally acceptance.

He'd done it before. The first time with Flor, more recently with Margaret.

The first one had been the real toughie, to Lyons's way of thinking. And the "why me" part, the "it's not fair, how could God let this happen," had taken a long time for even the Ironman to get through.

He *had* gotten through it, though. And, with the peculiar Ironman strength, he had emerged all the stronger for it.

It wasn't that he shut down his emotions. It was more a gradual process of coming to understand that nobody—including God, if He existed—owed Lyons an explanation. *Why* didn't matter. To cry out that it wasn't fair didn't matter. It only prolonged the agony, and deflected his grief from where it should be, namely missing her and healing.

What mattered was that, fair or not, it had happened.

Mourning was all right. It was part of acceptance, which was in turn part of getting over it. But anger was destructive.

Learn a lesson from the trees, Ironman. Bend, don't break.

Moreover, in a strange, abstract way, Lyons regarded it as less a tragedy that Julie was killed at the airport than it was that the other people had died there also.

His reasoning was that of a professional soldier. And he had the objectivity to apply it to his love. Julie, he reasoned, had also been a soldier, of sorts. She had volunteered, and to some extent had assumed the risk in so doing.

The other people who were victims hadn't taken on that risk. They had been drafted, so to speak.

Especially the children. God, he hated it when children died. A child's coffin was so pitifully small.

He and Julie had once talked about the hazards they faced. Each knew the other could be killed, and each had decided to go for it anyway. The irony was that Lyons had implicitly assumed that he would be the one to eat the big one first, just because of the nature of Able Team's work.

None of this meant that he took her death in stride. He didn't. He went through the "why me" part. But it didn't kill him. It didn't paralyze him. As Brognola has suspected, he would in fact handle it in his own way.

There was one more thing on his mind, as well.

If he were really lucky, Lyons realized, he might get a shot at the bastards who did it to her.

Gadgets got the triggermen. Maybe Lyons could get the man who gave the nod.

That wouldn't be all bad, at that. The tree would bend a little, but then it would snap back and deliver one hell of a blow to the men responsible.

Lyons knew it wouldn't bring her back, of course.

But it would help bring him back.

9

A long rectangular table made of dark walnut occupied the main area of the conference room.

The table had a sort of character of its own. Somehow, it had the feeling of "the old soldier" about it, not "old" in the sense of "too old," but rather in the sense of being a veteran, a war-horse. Its surface bore nicks and scars of heavy usage, yet was still polished to a sheen.

"I've seen things and done things," it seemed to say. "I've survived the wars that have been, and will survive that that will come." Somehow, the table seemed to belong in that conference room.

It was rumored the table had once been in the office of the Secretary of Defense in Washington, D.C.

The story went that Brognola had appropriated it—"liberated" it, in the words of U.S. Government Service—for himself and had transferred it to Stony Man Farm when the facility was built. Or maybe it was from a conference room used by the Secretary, rather than his office. Nobody really knew for sure, and Brognola wouldn't tell.

Still, the table's authenticity was never doubted by most of those who had seen it and had heard the story.

In its presence history had been made. And until the big one dropped it would continue to be so. The heavy walnut piece conveyed a sense of sardonic durability that somebody had once compared to Winston Churchill. Standing firm, meeting the world's worst challenges head-on—a cigar clamped in the jaw, perhaps—until being finally leveled by time and biological failure.

The carpeting in the room was of durable nylon, sort of midway between orange and brown, with a short, tough nap. The walls were off-white. A large round clock was mounted over the door. It had black hands for the hours and minutes, and a red sweep-second hand. The digits were plain Arabic numerals.

"Like the clocks in my fucking grammar school," Lyons had once commented.

That clock had been there as long as anybody could remember. At the other end of the room, however, was a new addition.

It was a map of the world, some four by ten feet in size. The ten-foot dimension ran horizontally. Above it, at positions corresponding to key cities around the world, digital clocks displayed the time according to the specific time zones.

Brognola didn't like the digital clocks.

He would have preferred round clocks with sweep-second hands, largely out of tradition. Aaron "the Bear" Kurtzman disagreed. He wanted digitals. And because he managed the computers that controlled the clocks—and since it really wasn't a major thing with Brognola—digitals they were.

The overall effect of the room was all business.

Gadgets and Blancanales were the first ones in the room. They had barely exchanged greetings when Lyons walked in.

At just under six feet and a solid one-ninety, the former L.A. policeman's physique could best be described as rugged, with a solid musculature that bespoke his considerable strength. He had blond hair and a strong, cleft jaw.

Today, though, he looked tired, drawn out. His expression was perhaps a bit grimmer than was characteristic. He also looked a little thinner than usual— one-ninety was on the low end of normal for him these days. In other respects, however, he looked pretty much the same as he always did.

To the eyes of those who knew him, one thing was unchanged. He still had that slightly aggressive bearing about him, a strong, ready-to-hit-hard-and-be-hit-hard way of moving.

Lyons had grown up in La Crescenta, a pleasant community just above the city of Glendale on the outskirts of Los Angeles. He had played football both at Crescenta Valley High and at Cal State Los Angeles.

As a freshman at Cal State, his size had been a problem. College ball was an entirely different league from high school, and a lot of good prep athletes couldn't quite make the step up. Lyons had shown potential, in that he was explosively fast, as well as tough.

But he was also light.

The bone structure had been there, of course. By then, he had pretty much attained his full height of five-eleven, give or take a fraction. And he had wide, square shoulders and a deep rib box. But he lacked the muscle mass, the meat on that frame for college ball.

At best, he was rangy. At worst, he was lanky.

In high school, he had played linebacker. He went out for that position his first year at State, trying out for the freshman team, or frosh, as it was called.

At the end of the first week of preseason, the defensive coach called him in to discuss his future with the Cal State football program. Coach Ross was an old Alabama boy with a solid paunch and three lifetimes of football experience.

"Lyons, I'm goin' to be tryin' you at DB," the coach had informed him. It was during the third week of practice, in early August.

"I want to play linebacker, Coach," the young man had replied.

Lyons knew that he had no bargaining position whatever. Sure, he had been good, a standout, in high school. But there were lots of good players, from lots of schools with good teams, trying out for the freshman squad. However, he was determined to make his position known, as respectively but firmly as he could.

He waited while the coach considered it. Then came the reply.

"You're too light, Lyons."

"Light isn't a problem for me, Coach. I make up for it in fast. You know I'm fast, Coach. And I hit hard. Nobody's been breakin' tackles on me."

He hesitated. Coach Ross didn't reply, so Lyons went on.

"Of course I'll play wherever you want me, Coach. I just don't feel that good about defensive back, that's all."

Coach Ross saw the sincerity and the desire in the young athlete's voice. If Lyons had come off as a smartass, or had pulled a prima-donna number, Ross would have canned him on the spot. But he could tell this kid wasn't like that.

"It's your body, son," he explained.

"What do you mean, Coach?"

"You're fast enough, all right. And I gotta admit you hit good. But you're too light to take that kind of punishment. Leastways, not in the long run. Better you work on bein' a good DB, and you might have a good shot at playing varsity."

Lyons tried to conceal his desperation. "Sure, I'm light, Coach. But I'm barely eighteen. And I'm gaining weight every week, even in spite of the running shi— stuff in practice."

Coach Ross arched a skeptical eyebrow at him. "You been puttin' on weight, boy, even with the runnin'?"

At that point, Lyons made a decision that would affect his future life forever. It was an instantaneous thing, but later he would swear that in that flash, he thought it and came up with the bottom line.

There was nothing wrong with being a defensive back, of course.

It took speed, and quickness. In many ways, it required more athletic ability than did linebacker. And, to be sure, the physical punishment, though considerable, was a hell of a lot less than at the linebacker slot. DBs—wiry, fast, durable guys—had a sort of appeal all their own.

But Lyons didn't want that.

He liked to hit. He liked the contact. He liked being poised behind the defensive line, eye on the quarterback, waiting for the play to explode. He liked sensing how the play would unfold, and reacting accordingly. Move forward, move laterally, and fill the gap. Stop the big play.

And he liked the satisfying feeling of a good, solid tackle. Body low, head up, face into the numbers on the ball carrier's jersey, the cablelike muscles of his neck taking the hit, the grunt of effort on the impact.

So he lied.

Or, more accurately, he didn't take advantage of the coach's implied opening to retract his statement, or at least back off from it. He reiterated to Coach Ross that he had been gaining weight, in spite of the two-a-day practices.

Lying was something Lyons never did. Until then, anyway.

He never lied to his parents, or to his teachers, or to the cops the one time, as a brash seventeen-year-old, he had gotten jammed up by LAPD the year before. It wasn't in his character. Or so he thought.

"Yeah, Coach. I'm up two pounds this week. I think I'm hitting a growing spell, or something."

Coach Ross regarded the young player speculatively. Then the coach did something that *he* never did, at least not when a player argued with him. He gave in. Partway, at any rate.

"All right, Lyons. I'll make a deal with you. What do you weight right now?"

"Now, Coach?"

"Yeah. Right now."

"Uh, one eighty-eight," the blond youth had answered, mentally tacking a good six pounds on to what his true weight was. "Stripped," he added earnestly.

"Well, I didn't think you weighed yourself in a fucking tuxedo, boy," Coach Ross observed with heavy sarcasm. "One eighty-eight, huh? You sure about that?"

"Yes, Coach," Lyons stammered.

"Well, Lyons, this'll be our deal. It's August right now. You hit two hundred by October first, and you're linebacker. If not, you're DB. I'll move you, even if it's midseason. That is, *if* you're even still on the team."

"October first?"

"Yeah. Of course, you still got to make the grade. I'm assumin' that. You get hurt, or can't cut the punishment, and you're out of the linebacker position. But even if you make it, I got to be convinced you'll survive. That means more size."

"Two hundred, huh, Coach?"

"Yep."

That night, Lyons was torn between guilt at his "misrepresentation," as he preferred to call it, despair at the eighteen-pound goal and determination to somehow make it. Then, in typical Ironman fashion, he went at it.

He did two things.

One, he vowed never to lie, or make that sort of misrepresentation ever again. And two, he vowed to hit two hundred pounds by October. Whether he could do it remained to be seen. But if he failed, it wouldn't be for lack of trying.

He abandoned the school weight room and joined one of the famed L.A.-based power gyms. No fancy chrome dumbbells, no carpets, no Universal machines, no Jacuzzi, and—in those days—no women in the workout area. Just squat racks, bench press racks and lat machines, Olympic sets and dumbbells that went up to one-eighty for each dumbbell.

He sought out the biggest men who worked out there, and consulted them for workout advice. These were power-lifters, not bodybuilders, men who were squatting in the six-hundred range and bench-pressing in the fours, even then.

Young Carl Lyons, one eye on the calendar and the other on the scale, got their advice. And he followed it.

The secret, they said, was a three-part combination. Diet right, lift right and sleep right.

He ate big meals, of course, but that wasn't enough. He started taking vitamins. Then he found a used, single-drive Hamilton Beach milkshake machine at a restaurant supply outlet, and bought it. With it he blended all manner of high-protein, high-carbohydrate drinks.

Usually the drinks took the form of a combination of milk, ice cream, honey, molasses and high-protein powder.

The result was a succession of viscous, goopy messes, no two alike. They were sticky and thick and cloying, but, gagging, he got them down. He knocked back desiccated liver tablets by the fistfuls, and took digestive enzyme capsules and liquid acidophilus to help maximize his body's use of all the food. He took mineral tablets. He got ten hours of sleep a night.

And he worked out.

Use only the basic exercises, the power-lifters told him. You don't care about a pretty physique—you need the pounds, they said. Do the lifts that work the major muscle groups. And, because you've already been lifting hard, though without a defined program, do them heavy, with low repetitions. Rest three to five minutes between sets—no fast burnout stuff.

When you're through with a workout, they said, even your bones should feel tired.

Lyons did what they said. And his bones did feel tired.

Full squats, the barbell held on the back of his shoulders, behind his neck, supported by his trapezius muscles. Five sets of five reps, all the way down, thighs breaking parallel, for the first month. The second month he did a pyramid sort of program, five reps for the first set, four for the second, three for the third, then two, then one, each set ten to fifteen pounds heavier than the last one.

And, after a careful warm-up on each lift, all the weights had to be heavy.

Bench presses, ditto. And lat pulls. And behind-the-neck presses. And upright rowing. And seated cable rowing. And heavy barbell curls. And neck resistance exercises.

That was it. No burnout sets for muscle definition. No assistance exercises for shape. No gut work—he got that in football practice. No running, apart from what he did in practice. No biceps isolation exercises like the bodybuilders did.

Just the big stuff.

The eating actually proved in some ways to be the hardest part. He felt full all the time, uncomfortably stuffed part of the time. But he started to grow. He started to gain in spite of the running and the sprints and the agility drills.

By September, he was one-ninety. Then the season started, and the emphasis in practice shifted from conditioning to skills and drills. That meant less running, less wearing off precious ounces he was gaining.

By the last week of September, he was one ninety-six. He also started the first game for the frosh team. At linebacker, and did a hell of a job.

By the deadline of October first, he was one ninety-seven and three quarters, almost one ninety-eight. He had played his second game at linebacker, and done even better than the first.

Coach Ross found him after practice on October first. The old footballer had a twinkle in his eye, but his voice was gruff.

"How's the body weight, Lyons?"

"Uh, real good, Coach. I'm feeling strong."

"Two hundred?"

"Right around there. Goes up and down a pound or two," Lyons added, trying to lay the groundwork for his alibi if he came up a tad light.

"Wanna jump on the scale?"

"Like this?" Lyons was suited out in practice gear, cleats, pads, pants.

"Sure." Coach Ross gave a careless wave of his hand.

Lyons did so. Suited up as he was, the body weight was two-thirteen.

Coach Ross shook his head. "Lyons, we figure your gear weighs fifteen pounds. That makes you a coupla pounds light."

Lyons grinned nervously. Surely the coach wouldn't yank him from the linebacker slot after those first two games, even if he was light. Hell, the other coaches wouldn't want that. The team was working well as a unit, and this would upset things.

Still, he couldn't be sure.

"Not this stuff, Coach," he replied, smiling widely. "It's light gear. Only weighs twelve pounds, in fact, the way I figure."

"That how you figure, boy?"

"Yessir, Coach."

For a long moment, Coach Ross surveyed the young man seriously. Then he grinned.

"Twelve pounds, my ass. But you played a coupla good games, Lyons. And you got a good attitude. Don't let it go to your head, boy, but attitude's important. And energy. You can 'complish a helluva lot with those two. Now, get the hell out of here and keep up the good work."

In a unique sort of way, that entire episode had been a key one for the young Carl Lyons.

It wasn't a turning point, exactly. Not in the literal meaning of the term. But it showed him a lot about himself and his abilities, both mental and physical.

His campaign to meet Coach Ross's deadline—literally a "campaign to gain"—became a model, a prototype, of his later actions and his approach to life in other endeavors besides athletics. It served him throughout college, then during his years with the LAPD, the Organized Crime Strike Force and, now most recently, with Stony Man Farm.

As Coach Ross had said, attitude was important. It was especially important when the going was the toughest, and all the other resources were gone.

Then it came down to attitude.

And now, years later, attitude was just as important as it had been then. Lyons knew it. Gadgets knew it. And Blancanales knew it.

Today, as Lyons entered the Stony Man conference room, both Gadgets and Blancanales noticed that he looked light. One ninety isn't exactly insubstantial, but the Ironman definitely was not as thick as he usually was. He looked, well, lean and rangy, and perhaps a little cruel, like a timber wolf.

Nobody made any expressions of sympathy about Julie. That had been done. Lyons had accepted the comradeship, but the rest was up to himself. The meeting was all business.

Brognola opened the manila folder before him.

"Let's get under way," he announced simply. His tone dispelled any doubt that this was serious.

"This—" he gestured at the folder "—is called the Lambda file. It was compiled by agents of the Federal Bureau of Investigation. It is the starting point of our mission.

"As you know, Lambda is the eleventh letter of the Greek alphabet, corresponding to the letter *L* in our alphabet. I don't know why it is called the Lambda File. The Bureau didn't grace us with that information."

He paused and looked at the clocks above the map at the end of the conference room.

"In a little less than forty-eight hours from now, a ghost train is going to leave San Diego."

He paused and looked around. Nobody inquired what he meant by the announcement. If any one of the three agents was surprised, he didn't show it.

Brognola continued. "You'll all be on it."

10

Nobody spoke.

Nobody asked what in hell a ghost train was. No eyebrows went up. Nobody even changed his expression.

Lyons and Gadgets sat on opposite sides of the massive old table. When Brognola began speaking, Lyons had been gazing straight ahead. Both his forearms were on the table, his hands together, fingers laced. His gaze was fixed on the opposite wall, beyond the table and behind Gadgets.

Gadgets, for his part, had been drawing geometric doodles on the side of his white Styrofoam coffee cup.

The Ironman's only movements had been the slow, alternate tightening then relaxing of his hands. Occasionally he would disengage the fingers on one hand and curl them into his palm, making a fist. Then, just as unobtrusively, he would relax the fist again. The whole process was so slow and deliberate that it would have passed largely unnoticed in most other settings.

When the chief made his announcement, Lyons hesitated only for a fraction of a second, then resumed the slow process, shifting the tension from one arm to the other.

Blancanales, who had been sitting with his arms folded over his chest, showed no expression whatsoever. And Gadgets simply made a slight frown and continued his drawing, although it took the form of block letters spelling the words, GHOST TRAIN.

Far from being upset at the indifference his men displayed, Brognola was secretly delighted by it.

Under other circumstances, their apparent lack of attention might have been a breach of protocol. In the military, for instance, the HMFIC—Brognola had picked up the term from Lyons, who said it was a commonplace label used in the LAPD to refer to Head Motherfucker in Charge—would demand a sit-up-and-look-sharp display of attention before even beginning a briefing. Most large corporations, for that matter, would demand likewise.

Stony Man Farm was different.

One of the perks of the largely thankless job of getting your ass shot off to protect people you didn't even know was a certain informality that would not be allowed elsewhere.

Brognola knew his men. They didn't have to be told to pay attention.

He also knew fighting men in general. And, in the manner of a good leader, he understood that their apparent indifference was all a part of the animal. If he had said, "You're going to ride that ghost train into hell and arrest the devil himself," the reaction would have been the same.

Ditto if he had added, "And only one of the three of you will survive it." It was all part and parcel of being a warrior.

The men of the Special Forces, or Seal Team Six, or the old Delta Force were just the most publicized examples of the species. But the traits were shared by all types of commandos.

Part of it was training. Part of it came from pride. And still a third part was courage, in the form of acceptance of danger.

The courage part was difficult to explain. But like the concept of obscenity, in the words of one U.S. Supreme Court Justice: "You can't define it, but you know it when you see it."

Courage, to these men, meant acceptance of the dangers.

Sure, it's dangerous, they might say. *So what?*

The risks—wounds, maiming, torture, the loss of life—were always there. That was a given. When one had courage, one first accepted the existence of the dangers, then went about doing the task at hand in spite of them.

"Grace under pressure," as Ernest Hemingway had defined it, "grace" meaning poise, or control, a lack of erratic behavior or immobilizing fear. And, in many ways, it was a good definition, at least for the men in the conference room that morning.

Whatever a ghost train might be, whatever dangers might lie underneath the chief's announcement, Lyons and Gadgets and the Politician were willing to take a shot at it. And despite whatever came at them, they would maintain their grace, their ability to act and react to accomplish their mission.

And maybe even to survive.

Maybe they would be able to, and maybe they wouldn't. But if they couldn't, if *this* one proved to be one too many, the one that got them, one thing was sure. Whatever killed them, it would not, repeat not, be the fact that they lacked courage, or folded under the pressure or the danger.

They waited for Brognola to tell them what a ghost train might be.

"A ghost train," continued the chief, after a suitable time to relish their studied indifference to his announcement, "is a train that doesn't exist."

Still no reaction from the three men. It was as if Brognola had been saying something as uninteresting and nonsurprising as, "Two plus two equals four," or "Some criminal defense attorneys are bigger crooks than their clients."

"It doesn't exist officially, that is. It is top secret, and its runs are unscheduled."

Here Gadgets interjected mildly. "Unscheduled, Chief?"

Brognola looked at him. "Why do you ask that?" he demanded, a trifle sharply.

Gadgets shrugged. "I'd have thought if it was some top-secret project, its runs would be highly scheduled. It is just that the schedules wouldn't be published, or known. They wouldn't appear on any manifest, for example, or on any list of trains being run."

"All right, all right," conceded Brognola. "Good point. I didn't say it right."

"No big deal, Chief."

But Brognola was looking at Able Team's resident genius with great interest. "Any other little tidbits of information about ghost trains you'd like to share with us?"

"Negative, Boss."

"You sure?"

"Positive. I wouldn't know a ghost train if I met one. I just made the deduction from what you said about them being top secret and unscheduled. That's all."

"All right." Brognola grinned. "I didn't realize this was a goddamn English class. I'll try to be more precise in the future."

Throughout this exchange, Blancanales and Lyons had maintained their silence. Finally, the Politician broke it.

"In the intelligence business," he observed to nobody in particular, "you take your leads where you find them."

"To be sure," agreed Brognola smoothly, taking control of the meeting once more. The attitude displayed by his men reassured him that they were, in fact, in fighting shape. If the mind is ready, the rest will follow.

As old Coach Ross—who was probably dead or in a rest home by now—would have observed, "Attitude is what counts."

Brognola plunged into the meat of the subject.

"Our ghost train is a secret convoy carrying nuclear fuel. The runs are relatively few in number, and each one is specially scheduled. Routes are cleared in the strictest secrecy. Not even the railways know all the details, other than that it's some government project."

"What sort of nuclear stuff do they carry?" inquired Gadgets, intrigued.

"It varies. Uranium, principally. However, the exact cargo depends on what's needed at the time, the particular mission, so to speak."

"Radioactive isotopes?" inquired Gadgets.

"Yes. For the most part, it's U-235."

"Fissionable stuff, then," rejoined the Able Team genius. "For reactors, I'd guess, rather than bombs."

"Generally, that's true."

Gadgets gave Brognola a searching look. "I don't like the sound of that," he commented.

"What do you mean?"

"Generally?" he repeated. "Does that mean this one's different?"

Brognola didn't answer him directly. Instead, he consulted a document from the file before him. "The Lambda train will contain—I can't begin to tell you how far beyond top secret this is—deuterium, tritium and lithium isotopes."

Gadgets stared at him. "Bullshit," he finally declared, his voice flat.

"No bullshit," rejoined Brognola.

Lyons finally stopped tensing his hands and looked up. "Question, Chief."

"Go ahead."

"With all due respect, would you two rocket scientists mind putting this in plain English for the benefit of the rest of us knuckle-draggers? You know, the guys who are going to be getting their asses shot at over this business?"

Brognola nodded. "That's fair enough," he allowed. He paused for a moment, collecting his thoughts, then began.

"We're talking about two kinds of nuclear reactions. One's called fission, and involves splitting atoms to release energy. The other is called fusion, which means combining, or fusing, two atoms together. You with me so far?"

Lyons nodded.

"Good. Now, both processes release energy. Tons of it. Like, the amount of energy that gets released results in an explosion."

"The atomic bomb, in other words?" pressed the Ironman.

"That's affirmative. An atomic bomb uses fission. That's what was used in Nagasaki and also in Hiroshima, and you know what happened there. Also, nuclear reactors—the kind in nuclear power plants—use a controlled, slowed-down fission to generate heat to make electricity."

"Makes sense so far. But what's all this 'E-equals-MC-squared' crap have to do with us?"

Brognola looked at his lead fighter with approval. "Very good, Ironman. Einstein would be proud of you. Hang on a sec and I'll tell you." He paused, then went on. "The other process, fusion, is used only for bombs."

Gadgets, seeing his partner's perplexity, interjected. "We're talking about H-bombs—hydrogen bombs—now. They're also called thermonuclear bombs," he added helpfully.

"Oh, yeah?" said Lyons. "Do tell."

Brognola winked. "Stand by, Ironman. This'll make sense in a moment. This fusion, the H-bomb process, releases several thousand times as much energy as fission. But the release is so fast and violent that it can't be controlled, and the only practical use so far is for the H-bomb."

Blancanales shook his head slowly. "Some practical use," he muttered sarcastically.

Lyons stared at Brognola, then at Gadgets. "So what you whiz kids are telling me is that the bombs we used on Japan were the lightweight kind? The kind that uses, uh..."

"Fission," Brognola agreed, nodding.

"Jesus," muttered Lyons.

"A hydrogen bomb has not yet been actually deployed against any enemy target yet," Brognola continued, "but they have actually been tested by the Soviet Union, China, France and Great Britain, in addition to the U.S., of course."

Lyons shook his head. His face wore a look of tiredness, a sort of sad fatigue. "I don't mean to sound like some tree-hugging, starry-eyed fucking dipshit liberal," he began, "but..."

"But what, Ironman?"

"It doesn't make sense, us and every other swinging dick big country in the world building these fuckers as fast as we can, especially these big bastards."

"No," Brognola agreed. "It doesn't make much sense."

Nobody responded.

"On the other hand, who's going to stop building them first? Us? You trust the Russians to stop if we stop?"

Lyons gave a quick shake to his head. "Too much for me to do anything about. That's for you big shots. How's all this affect us patrol jockeys, anyway?"

"What Gadgets was saying, or I said, actually," Brognola replied, "is that the Lambda train is carrying the nuclear materials for the big bastards, as you call them. The thermonuclear bombs."

All indifference had vanished. The three commandos looked intently at Brognola. The chief returned the gaze of each man in turn. When he spoke, his voice was deadly serious.

"What I'm saying is that you three will be on that train. To put it bluntly, you'll be riding shotgun on enough nuclear material to build the biggest goddamn H-bomb the world has yet seen."

He paused for a moment.

"And...the train is going to be hijacked."

11

Brognola consulted the file before him, the file that Julie had died holding.

The Lambda file.

"This train leaves San Diego the day after tomorrow. Its destination is Oak Ridge, Tennessee. And it is in fact carrying the ingredients for an H-bomb.

"We know it is going to be hijacked. That's where you come in."

Nobody had to be told what the team's purpose was going to be. Or what kind of welcome they would be expected to give the hijackers.

"Question, Chief." It was Blancanales who spoke.

"Go ahead."

"Who's going to be doing the hijacking?"

Brognola shook his head. "It's a new group. We don't know much about them. They call themselves the New World Insurrectionists."

"Fuck," Lyons muttered disgustedly.

"What is it, Lyons?"

The Ironman shook his head. "New World Insurrectionists. What a crock of shit. The legacy of Che Guevara lives on."

"How so?"

"Back in the sixties, every long-haired, far-left radical had a poster of Che on the wall of his dorm room. The liberator of Cuba. The guerrilla warfare genius. And they all formed their own little cults, the 'People's Insurgency this,' the 'Insurrectionist Underground that.'" He paused and looked up at Brognola. "And you know what?"

"Go ahead, Carl." The chief's voice was softer this time. "What?"

"Every one of those goddamn left-wing, free-the-people groups was just as rigid, and unforgiving, and dictatorlike as the worst of the governments they sought to overthrow." Lyons stopped suddenly. A look of embarrassment crossed his face. "Sorry, guys," he said sheepishly.

It was Blancanales who responded. "No sweat, amigo," he said with an easy grin. "We actually studied some of Señor Guevara's guerrilla philosophies in the army. But as a kid, I also got my fill of that kind of hero worship."

"Well, sorry for spouting off."

Gadgets gave him a keen look. "If I may say so, Ironman, this heavy political philosophy shit isn't usually your bag. What's—"

Lyons cut him off. His response was partly an answer and partly a message that he didn't want to talk about it further.

"I was peripherally involved in a deal the LAPD Intelligence Division was doing back then. Worked with the FBI on the Weather Underground," he said vaguely. "Spent some time hanging out at UCLA and listening to the likes of Angela Davis and the rest of the pseudorevolutionaries."

"No sweat, Homes," said Gadgets. "I was just curious, that's all."

"It just seems sort of demeaning."

"Demeaning how?"

"To get blown away by some group whose name sounds like a bunch of amateur student radical dipshits spouting Marxism at the campus coffee shop." Lyons shook his head again, the look of fatigue creeping around the corners of his eyes. "Although you're just as dead either way, I guess."

Brognola took over again. "If that's your concern, Ironman, forget it."

Lyons looked at him, but didn't speak.

"This group, the New World Insurrectionists, are anything but amateur. Their commandos have been trained by some of the top—if I may use that word—terrorist organizations in the world, among them some of the most secret PLO camps. They'll be well armed, well disciplined and utterly willing to give up their lives in the service of their cause.

"Following the tradition of the original terrorists—the eleventh-century Persians—they believe it is noble, even desirable, to die in the service of their cause. And—" here Brognola felt a pang at his earlier speculation of what might happen if Lyons flipped out over Julie's death "—I don't have to tell any of you how dangerous is the trained soldier who doesn't care if he dies, or even wants to die, as long as it's in a battle."

"Question, Chief," said Gadgets.

"Shoot."

"Who's behind them?"

Brognola nodded. "Good point. I was getting to that. The NWI themselves are the actual soldiers, the enforcement arm, so to speak. They'll be the guys who actually do the hijacking."

"But they're actually controlled by somebody else?"

"That's affirmative. The CIA has established—to the satisfaction of the President, at least—that the New World Insurrectionists are funded and controlled by the Soviet Union."

Lyons spoke up. "How do you know about this, anyway?"

"What do you mean?"

"Well," the Ironman responded, irritation in his voice, "the NWI certainly doesn't hold public meetings. How do we know all of this, especially their plans to hijack the Lambda train? We have a snitch into them, or what?"

Brognola winced slightly. Then he took refuge behind official double-talk. "For present purposes, let us, ah, assume there is an informant in the group, as you suggest. I can assure you that I, at least, am satisfied the information is accurate and reliable."

Lyons pressed on. "Are these NWI bastards Russians themselves? Or are they radical dupes being used by the Russians to do their dirty work?"

"No," said Brognola simply.

"No what?"

"No, the NWI are not Russians themselves. They probably don't even know the Soviets are pulling their strings. And the Soviet Union's control is probably insulated, hidden, by a couple of layers of 'front' activist groups."

Lyons nodded.

Brognola grimaced, then went on. "You know the story. Russian money, controlled by a Russian case agent, is given anonymously to this cause, who controls that cause, who, in turn, runs the NWI. A good case agent can then play with the purse strings and direct the NWI to do its bidding."

"And in this case," Gadgets asked, "that bidding is?"

"To get their hands on the H-bomb materials. Or at least to make a hell of a good try at it."

It was Blancanales who finally broke the silence that lasted for several moments after this pronouncement. "There's one thing I don't understand."

"Only one?" asked Brognola.

"What are these NWI guys going to do with the stuff if they are able to pull it off?"

"What do you mean?"

"Well, they must know that they're in for a hell of a manhunt if they do this. And for what? Can they actually build a bomb? Can they expect to do so before they get caught?" He shook his head. "I don't understand, tactically speaking, what they ultimately hope to accomplish."

"Very, very good," observed Brognola. "An interesting point, wouldn't you say? And one that I've given considerable thought to resolving."

"And?" prompted the Politician.

The Stony Man Chief of Operations spoke deliberately, choosing his words carefully. "I believe that if the CIA is correct, and if the Russians are behind this, that it doesn't matter what they are going to do with the thermonuclear materials."

The Politician looked at him. "How so?"

"Their main mission, I believe—or, to be more precise, the main mission of those who control them—is not necessarily to obtain the nuclear material. It is to *try* to get the nuclear stuff."

"All right," Lyons said sarcastically. "You've lost me. Would you mind explaining that?"

Brognola nodded. "Sure. The Soviet Union wins either way. If the NWI pulls it off and gets its hands on those isotopes, even temporarily, it will be media sensation. 'Terrorists Seize U.S. H-Bomb,' blah, blah, blah. You can just imagine the headlines."

"So what are you saying, Chief?"

"Well, the same thing will happen if they even come close. The press will pick up on the fact the government was transporting H-bomb materials. There'll be stories on how easily the hijacking could have been successful. Somebody will propose a congressional inquiry, and all the antidefense demonstrators will have more grist for their mill."

The chief of Stony Man Operations looked around the room. "In short, that part of Soviet strategy that consists of feeding the antigovernment sentiment in this country will have been advanced, no matter whether they get the isotopes or not."

"And if they are successful..." Blancanales thought aloud.

"If they do get the stuff, so much the better. They'll try to build a bomb themselves, or get it to Cuba. Hell, I don't know."

"Maybe they'll offer to give it back if the U.S. makes some concessions," Gadgets suggested. "Frees some so-called political prisoners, or some bullshit like that."

Brognola nodded. "Could be. Whatever they do with it, though, is secondary to the main mission. And the CIA believes, as I do, that the main mission is simply to make one hell of a good try."

Lyons thought it over. He had to admit it made sense, particularly if the NWI commandos didn't mind a suicide mission.

Still, something didn't quite add up. Something tugged at the corners of his mind. And, though normally he didn't think of himself as particularly intuitive—he'd leave that to Gadgets—Lyons trusted his cop instincts enough not to completely ignore the nagging thought.

Mentally, he reached for whatever it was, but it eluded him.

He became aware the others were looking at him. Maybe his expression had given him away. Brognola, in fact, confirmed it.

"That make sense, Lyons?" he inquired.

"Yeah, it does."

"You look like something rang a bell for you. Anything on your mind about this?"

Knowing it was futile, the Ironman made one last mental grab for the elusive idea. Then he shook his head. "Nothing right now, Chief. I'll have to think on it."

Brognola looked around the table. "Anybody else?"

For a few moments, nobody voiced an opinion. Then Gadgets spoke up. Out of consideration for Lyons, he chose his words and the tone of his voice carefully, trying to be at once neutral and compassionate.

"After Julie was shot, she managed to say a name to me. 'Axis Powers,' she said." He looked at Brognola. "We discussed it on the telephone before that little bit of excitement yesterday."

"I remember."

"Is there any connection between that and this caper?"

Brognola seemed to be both nodding and shaking his head at the same time. "Good point," he said, and the others realized that the nod went with that statement, rather than what followed it. "But the answer is no. At least, not yet, anyway."

"Could it be a reference to the terrorists, the New World Insurrectionists?" pressed Gadgets.

"I know what you mean," Brognola said. "It sounds like a political term. And of course, it is a political concept, political in the international sense.

And..." Seeing the puzzled look on Lyons's face, he left the sentence unfinished.

"Excuse my ignorance," said the Ironman, "but what does it mean?"

Brognola nodded to Gadgets, who responded. "It's the name that was given to the countries who sided together against the Allies in World War II. Germany, Italy and Japan, to be exact."

"Oh."

The Chief took over. "We've searched all over hell to find some connection. Like maybe it would show who was backing the New World Insurrectionists, or who they were, or give us something to work on."

"And?"

"All results negative. Zippo. We can't find any link between that term and the terrorists, or the bomb, or the train, or anything."

"A code word, maybe?" speculated the Politician.

Brognola looked at him. "Like what?"

"I don't know. I'm just brainstorming. But if 'Axis Powers' had something to do with Japan, maybe it has something to do with the bomb."

"Explain that."

"Well, the atomic bomb was first used on Japan, right? That was its first military deployment. Maybe it relates to the materials for the atomic bomb, the materials that are on the train." He paused, and looked around with a rueful smile. "Only thing is, I can't imagine how in the hell it would possibly tie in."

Gadgets and Brognola variously shrugged and shook their heads in bewilderment.

"It's as good a theory as any," the Chief said at last. "I'll turn Kurtzman loose on it, see what he can come up with."

"Say," Lyons interjected suddenly.

"What is it, Ironman?"

"Maybe it's not a term at all."

"Huh?" Gadgets, for once, looked perplexed.

"Look," said Lyons. "You kept calling it—Axis Powers—a 'name.' The Chief keeps referring to it as a 'term,' or a 'concept.' There's a difference."

"So what?"

"Well, I'm just a dumb cop, not some fucking political scientist like you guys. But I've interviewed a hell of a lot of witnesses and crooks before I got hooked up with this outfit. And..." He hesitated, searching for the right way to express what he wanted to say.

The others waited.

"And I know that a lot of times people say names differently than they say words that aren't names. Terms, if you want to call them that." He turned to Gadgets. "Could it have been a name?"

"A name?"

"Yeah. Somebody's name. Not a code word or some fucking political term, but a name. You called it a 'name' when you asked the chief about it. Could she have been trying to give you a man's name?"

"Axis doesn't sound much like a man's name," Brognola said gently. "It could be, Carl, but frankly—"

Lyons interrupted him. "I had a murder case when I was with the cops where the suspect was named Bob Wevel. His nickname, of course, was Boll Weevil. But if I were in a room full of people, and I was trying to say 'boll weevil' as a name it would probably sound a little different than if I wanted to talk about goddamn cotton plants."

Gadgets was intrigued.

He liked this sort of metaphysical puzzle as much as he did playing with computers or electronics. "I *did* call it a name, didn't I?" he mused. He shut his eyes and, in his mind, put himself back into the pandemonium of the airport, where he knelt and cradled a dying woman in his arms. Still, he couldn't recreate the moment.

Lyons looked at him, questioningly. Gadgets shrugged.

"The best I can say is that if I called it a name, maybe subconsciously it was because she maybe said it like a name. But at this particular moment, I can't say for sure."

"Hypnosis?" suggested the Politician.

Brognola interrupted. "No need for that. I'll just go on the assumption it might be a name, and tell the Bear to go after it on that theory as well. We have nothing to lose, anyway. And who knows? We just might hit something."

The tone of his voice indicated he didn't hold much hope, but he'd go through the motions anyway. The others sensed this was a dead issue, and remained silent.

Then the Stony Man Operations Chief looked around. "If nobody else has any ideas, let's take a look at the operational aspects of this thing."

The Politician winked. "You mean the layout of the shooting gallery where we'll be the ducks."

"Right. That's what I said. The operational aspects. Actually, that part is relatively simple." Brognola closed the Lambda file as if to affirm that the complicated stuff was over. "The theory behind the train is to have it lightly guarded. The guards are well trained—by normal standards—civilians who have been cleared by all the pertinent commissions. The theory is to travel light to avoid the suspicion that a major entourage inevitably attracts."

He paused and looked at the three men.

Even as he talked another voice spoke silently inside his mind. "Sure the operational aspect is relatively simple," the voice said, "simple to say, that is. But it'll be damned hard to survive."

The Stony Man chief suddenly wondered if he would ever see these three men alive again. Then, as their general, he put the thought away. It had to be this way.

"You three will be substituted for three of the guards on the Lambda train. We don't know how the hijack will work, but we hope to have that information shortly, courtesy of the informant.

"You'll ride the train into whatever trap they have set for you. And, when they spring it, you'll try your best to shoot your way out of it and hang on to the thermonuclear materials."

Almost unconsciously, Lyons stepped back into his role as Able Team's leader. It was he alone who spoke. "Try our best," he repeated.

"Yes," said Brognola, his voice expressionless. "That's what guards do, isn't it?"

"Yeah. I guess it is."

"And ducks, for that matter," the chief added wryly.

Lyons nodded. "Ducks, too," he agreed. There didn't seem to be much else to say.

12

Vince didn't like it one bit.

Professionally speaking, he prided himself on two things. One was planning, the other secrecy. In one sense, of course, the two were intertwined. Careful planning helped maintain secrecy, and maintaining secrecy was always a major part of his planning. But now, it was beginning to seem as if both might have been shot in the ass.

Fatally compromised, in other words.

Careful planning, he believed, required an objective assessment of the situation. You gotta figure out what's fucking what, he liked to say, no 'yes-man' bullshit. Good news or bad, he wanted the truth.

He went over the facts in his mind. As always, he was careful to recognize the facts that he *knew* to be true—those that had been verified by independent evidence—and those that he merely thought were true.

The first item, one that he knew to be true, was that Rafe was dead.

That alone would be distressing under any circumstances. But today, on the eve of the biggest single Mafia operation ever undertaken, the loss of his trusted gunsel had turned an already tense situation into a virtual crisis.

Rafe had been in many respects his best man.

This was particularly so in the area of enforcement. When you couldn't go to the law to keep people in line, Vinnie knew, you had to have an alternative approach. Within the West Coast Mafia, particularly Los Angeles northward, Vince Danelli was the law of the mob, and Rafe had been his chief marshal.

It happens all the time, Vince thought.

A dope courier finally succumbs to the temptation of going into business for himself—why settle for a piss-ant five hundred bucks to make this delivery when he's got twenty or thirty thousand bucks of the mob's dope?

So he makes himself brave and rips off the dope. In a surprising number of cases there is a woman behind it, somebody the guy wants to impress, somebody who makes him brave. Maybe he goes into hiding until he's pissed through the money, or he tries to say the dope was stolen from him.

Either way, the mob's gotta stop it.

Or take a pimp, or an L.A. bookie who starts working a side business. The dude's not exactly stealing from the organization, not really. He's just running his own little enterprise, right alongside the one he's running for them. *These* are the mob's hookers, and *these* are my own, he says. *These* are the mob's bettors, and these over here are mine.

Mob doesn't like that, either. Free enterprise may be cool, but not in that context.

All these things cropped up from time to time. Not really frequently, but with some degree of regularity nonetheless. And when they did, Vince Danelli had to put a stop to it.

Vince was a very bright guy. Sometimes, he talked like the Mafia hood that he was, and sometimes he sounded like a Harvard lawyer. And when these enforcement problems cropped up, he showed both.

"What is needed," he would ruminate, "is some deterrent activity."

Rafe, who had been used to this split-personality quirk in his boss, would listen patiently.

"Yes, Rafe, our action must accomplish multiple objectives. We need to reform the offender. We need to encourage him to adopt proper business loyalties in the future. And..."

"How bad do you want me to fuck him up, boss?"

"Please. Let's not put it in those terms. I was about to say that whatever sanction we impose must be such that it will communicate to others the attitude that disloyalty to us is a crime of sorts and will not be tolerated."

"How bad do you want me to fuck him up, boss?"

And Vince Danelli would think, and pass sentence. "I want you to blast his fucking kneecaps, Rafe," he would say, or whatever else he thought was appropriate to fix the particular case.

For the past six years, Rafe had been the man who actually did the fixing. He was, Vince knew, utterly fearless, and just as tough as he was brave.

Cool bastard, too.

Sometimes he killed them. Sometimes he just broke them a little. Maybe bent an elbow backward, the wrong way, until it popped and broke. If it was to be a kill job, there were various ways to do that, too. Neatly, if the guy deserved mercy, maybe by putting a couple of clean ones in the head. Or painfully, if that was more appropriate.

Either way, Rafe was the man.

Moreover, so far as Vince could tell, Rafe had had no designs on moving up the organization. To be sure, he had been paid substantially more than most muscle. In fact, he had lived quite well. But his income had still been less than the rewards he would have gotten had he graduated to a middle-management position in the mob. Yet Rafe had been content where he was.

And now he was nowhere.

"Mother-fuck!" The Mafia-hood side of Vince was showing. He spit the oath as he slammed down the heel of his hand on the sheet of glass that covered the desk in his sumptuous Los Angeles office.

Who *were* those bastards? he wondered for the hundredth—or was it the thousandth—time.

Vinnie Danelli was worried.

He was glad nobody else was in the room to see his outburst. "The Iceman," they all called him. "Cool Vinnie." The man who never raised his voice, who spoke even more quietly and softly as the stress increased. Usually, that is.

For an instant he wondered if he was losing it.

Angrily, he grabbed again the four pages of single-spaced typing that described the autopsy performed on the late, unfortunate Rafe. The top page bore the official seal of the Los Angeles County Coroner, and a stamp across the front read, Confidential—For Law Enforcement Use Only. Contents not to be divulged elsewhere without court order.

Wasn't that the fucking limit, he thought bitterly. Only the cop-type words were capitalized. The rest of the sentence—including the word "court"—was not.

Fucking cops, he thought.

A telephone call to the right source had resulted in a copy of the report hand-delivered to him three days after the pathologist's dictation had been typed.

As he once again scanned the report, it occurred to him that he already knew what it said. He knew it by heart, in fact, ditto on those dealing with Joey and Hal and Randy.

But Rafe's took the cake.

He found and read the subparagraph entitled Summary and Conclusions.

> Primary cause of death, loss of brain function due to massive head injuries due to gunshot wounds entering brain area. Secondary cause of death, not applicable; though head injuries would be likely to result in sufficient blood loss to produce death by exsanguination, this conclusion not listed as contributing factor due to instantaneous nature of death from primary cause.

Elsewhere the report described the gunshot wounds themselves. All four of them.

Four! And all in the side of the head, fired at a moving vehicle with the window rolled up.

And Joey, dead from a single slug in the gut. Hal, who had taken two or three—the pathologist couldn't be sure which—also in the head. And Randy, with one in the head.

Who *were* those bastards?

The only survivor of his hit team, that psycho spick Sebastian, said there had only been two of them. Two! That two men could take out his first team was unsettling enough. But on the eve of the biggest caper ever...

One guy sounded like the dude Rafe described at the airport. It had to be the same guy, in fact, because Rafe had him under surveillance the whole time, until the others arrived.

"Ordinary-looking fucker, boss," Sebastian had said. "To tell you the truth, I can't really remember what he looked like."

"Try," Vince had urged him softly, but there was no mistaking the softness for gentleness. "How tall was he?"

"Well, he wasn't real tall, boss. And he wasn't real short, either. So I guess he was average."

"How old was he?"

"Well, he wasn't a kid, and he wasn't no old dude, either."

And on and on it went, not much help. The guy had on tan clothes. And could jump, he jumped over their car, for Christ's sake. And he iced the guys at the airport, and at least a couple of the guys in the hit car.

And the second guy? Vince had inquired of Sebastian.

Not much help there, either.

It seems they had the first guy in sight, the guy with the briefcase. And then, right when they were moving in to make the crunch and grab the briefcase, this second guy shows up. Must've been the one the first guy was talking to on the phone.

So, what did he look like? Vince had inquired.

A beaner, said Sebastian. And Christ, thought Danelli, Sebastian ought to know. But the guy was clean-cut looking, not like some gangster. Stocky. Some gray in his hair. And, like the first guy, driving a rented car.

According to Sebastian, that was the guy that got Rafe so solid. Four fucking times worth of solid.

Another thing disturbed Danelli.

Afterward, after all the shooting and the cops and the FBI and the press falling all over one another, the two dudes had flat vanished. And now, despite an intensive investigation, nobody seemed to know who they were.

The papers called them "mystery figures in the gangland gun battle." But the inside word was that nobody in the news had a line on who they were. Vinnie's sources in the LAPD didn't know any more than that. And, said his sources, the FBI didn't know, either. Or at least, he amended, those sources said the Bureau was doing a lot of asking around about who those guys were, which could be a ruse or could be for real.

Vinnie tended to think it was for real.

So, who were they?

They weren't cops. And they weren't Feebies.

And a more important question was why? Why were they at the airport, the average-looking guy, anyway? What were they up to? Specifically, what was their interest in the briefcase that the FBI broad had been carrying? Especially if they weren't FBI themselves.

"Mother-fuck." He growled it this time.

Danelli rose to his feet and crossed the spacious office. He opened the doors to a dark walnut cabinet and removed a bottle of expensive, single-malt Scotch. Splashing a generous slug into a heavy, cut-glass tumbler, he walked back to his desk.

He liked his booze the way he liked his women—neat. Or smooth.

The smooth, hot liquid calmed him a little. It helped him focus on the real question, the one that was the cause of all his anxiety.

Were these guys on to the train caper?

He took another drink of the Scotch, and reflected that in almost every respect, the train caper scared him.

First was the fact that all their eggs were, so to speak, in that one basket. That was great, of course, if the basket came through without damage. The problem, as always, was that if they lost—if that basket failed or got misplaced or dropped or broken—they lost big. Real big.

Vince Danelli, the planner, didn't like working like that. He liked to diversify, to hedge, to have several baskets.

Unfortunately, he didn't have a choice in this instance. The head man himself had made that clear. The plan had been hatched by others, then dropped into Vinnie's lap with a big red Don't Fuck Up label all over it.

So he had to try to carry out somebody else's brainchild, and that somebody happened to be none other than the head man, Mr. A., as they liked to call him. Or, more formally, Mr. Powers.

The pressure was on Vince Danelli, and he knew it. When Mr. Powers himself was making the hand-off, Vince Danelli better not fumble the ball.

Then, too, he had to work with those fucking terrorist crazies. The New World somebodies. Absolute fanatics. Total, stone-psycho assholes, who were going to actually pull off the heist for them.

And, in so doing, enable the Mafia to pull off the biggest one-shot deal they had ever done, *if* the head man's plan worked as it was supposed to....

13

Actually, Vinnie reflected, working with the New World crazies might prove in some respects to be the best part of the boss's plan, the train caper.

Correction. Make that *his* plan, now that the boss had dumped it in his lap.

Moreover, if it turned out that the two guys who wasted Rafe and the others were, by some extreme stretch of the imagination, law enforcement types who were going to try to block the caper, Vinnie now had the perfect solution. Throw the New World maniacs at them, and let them fight it out.

He felt better just thinking of it.

For one thing, the crazies were good fighters. Damn good fighters. Rafe said they were the best he had ever seen. He'd told Vince that their training was equal to the Green Berets, for God's sake, though they had gotten it at some Middle Eastern terrorist camps or some such bullshit.

For another thing, they were expendable. And, not only were they expendable, but they knew it.

That was weird.

Sure, they didn't actually want to get caught. They didn't want to die. Other things being equal, they would like to pull this one off in the name of world peace—incidentally killing a bunch of civil servant guards and engineers in the process—and get safely away to repeat the act somewhere else. But if they get caught or killed, no big deal.

They wouldn't squeal if they were caught. And they didn't care about getting killed.

In fact, they acted as if dying or getting captured was almost as good as staying alive and killing people. Both were just different ways of serving their cause. And, regardless of how loony Vince thought their cause was, *they* believed in it.

Fanatics.

He couldn't understand it, but he knew what it meant to him, strategically speaking.

This do-or-die-trying attitude provided an added tactical dimension to the operation. And it was this edge that led Vinnie to believe that he might still pull it off, despite what happened to Rafe and the others.

He regarded this tactical dimension as vital.

Normally, he knew, in planning an operation of this sort, considerable attention had to be given to the safety of your men. This was true even if your men were thugs and killers, who accepted a certain degree of risk that they could get hurt. You still had to keep that risk at an acceptably low level. The men simply expected it. Union rules, so to speak.

Unlike whatever causes the New World maniacs believed in, the traditional Mafia causes were more on the material side—greed and money and power.

Traditional, all-American values.

However, these weren't usually regarded as being worth one's life, especially since the risk of getting convicted and going to jail was fairly low. Even with honest judges, the system was so weighted in favor of the crooks that their attorneys were often able to dick the case around enough to beat the vast majority of the raps.

The law, he reflected, was a marvelous thing for people in his line of work.

Vince Danelli and most of his cohorts had learned to become ardent supporters of constitutional rights. They gave generous donations to the American Bar Association and several other judges' and lawyers' groups.

The donations, of course, had the added benefit of being tax deductible.

So the modern Mafia attitude had become, why risk dying if the chief consequences of failure were a little jail time and a big lawyer's bill? Those were all part of the game. And this attitude put certain danger limits on their tactics in a mission like this one.

But these New World assholes weren't like that.

Of course, it took a while for Vince to really understand why these guys didn't particularly worry about death or imprisonment. But when he'd grasped the concept a whole new world appeared before him, operationally speaking.

Vinnie had, in fact, discussed the concept with Rafe shortly after Mr. A. had dumped the mess in his lap.

The discussion had at first been in general terms, of course—Rafe, though trusted, had nonetheless been only a gunsel. Accordingly, Vinnie had confined their talk to specific tactical considerations.

Initially, Rafe had shared his skepticism.

"I dunno, Vinnie. It just don't make sense these guys ain't worried about bein' killed or captured."

"I agree. It doesn't make sense. But just think if it was true."

"What do you mean, Vinnie?"

"Just suppose you've got men on your side, soldiers, that the only thing you care about is how to use them to kill the other side. Just think of the possibilities."

Rafe didn't reply, so Danelli went on.

"Say, for example, we were trying to take down another guy. Just an example, Rafe. And say the other guy had a pistol, a .45, and all we had was two or three men with knives, no guns."

"Don't sound too good for us, then."

"No, it doesn't. But if our men, the two or three guys with knives, don't care if they get killed or caught—I mean really just don't give a damn at all—then it's no problem, is it?"

Rafe looked skeptical. Danelli went on.

"Your guys, they just fan out and they charge the guy with the gun. One of 'em goes high and two go low. Do you see what I'm saying?"

Rafe nodded thoughtfully. "Yeah, Vinnie. That's a fact. You lose one, maybe two, but you'll get the fucker with the piece."

Vince Danelli nodded. "That's right, Rafe. That's damn well right. If you don't have to worry at all about your men, you can do a lot more toward accomplishing your goal."

"Like the Chinks," Rafe said at last.

"The Chinks?"

"You know. Chinese."

"I know, Rafe. What about them?"

"Those stories about the Red Chinese or whatever they are, where they got so many millions of guys, an' life don't mean shit anyway, they just keep chargin' a machine gun until the bastard breaks down or overheats or whatever."

Vince nodded. Rafe went on.

"Or until the stiffs are piled so fuckin' high the machine gun can't be angled up enough to shoot over the bodies. Then they overrun the gunner and cut him to pieces."

Vince shrugged. Rafe was quick to grasp the practical application, all right. And there was a certain parallel.

"Yes, I guess so. Only we won't have that many, of course, so we can't actually do that. But it's the same idea. And besides, in real life, our guys won't have just knives, they'll have Uzis and grenades. Hell, they'll be as well or better armed than the guys they're goin' up against."

Rafe thought a moment longer. "There's somethin' else, too," he said quietly.

"What's that?"

"If a guy ain't afraid to die, he does better in other ways, too."

"What do you mean?"

Vinnie looked at Rafe in genuine interest. His best enforcer was by no means simply an all-brawn-and-no-brains knuckle dragger. Still, he normally wasn't given to deep insights. Or, if he had them, he kept them to himself. Yet something in his tone this time was significant.

"It's hard to say exactly. But the guy would be more effective in a lotta ways. Not just in what you use him for, but in how he does whatever he's doing. You know what I mean?"

"Yeah, Rafe. I know what you mean."

"Like, you can use him for more stuff, sure, but also he's better at everything. 'Cause his mind ain't distracted by coverin' his ass."

Vinnie nodded. Good point, and one that only a guy like Rafe—who had been there himself—would come up with.

Then his gunsel spoke again. "You really think they are like this, or are they just talkin' some heavy bullshit?"

"I honestly don't know," Danelli replied with rare candor. "It seems like it's for real, though." Then an idea occurred to him. "I'd like you to check them out, though. Just talk to 'em. See what you think. After all, if this plan comes off, you'll be my man in charge on the scene."

So they had done that.

They had arranged, through Mr. A. himself, for Rafe to meet the squad leaders of the New World Insurrectionists. The meeting took place in some rugged wasteland in Mexico, and when Rafe came back, he was impressed.

"I've never seen anythin' like it, Vinnie," he'd reported.

"They're for real, then?"

"They're for real. And you know what else?"

"Tell me."

"Their leader's a broad."

Vince had stared at his gunsel in disbelief. "A *what*?" he demanded, as if he didn't know what one was.

"A broad. Calls herself Kara."

"Jesus!" Vince was stunned.

"A broad, Vince," Rafe repeated. "Honest to God—"

"She have big tits?" Danelli interrupted crudely. "What is she, some blond, six-foot fucking Amazon with big tits?"

It came out as a crude sneer, his question invoking the characteristics he and many of his Mafia cohorts regarded as the most important attributes of a woman.

"Nope. Not this—"

"Maybe," Vince interrupted again, "we could use her in Vegas when this is all over. Stick her in one of the floor shows, you know what I mean?" He laughed harshly.

"Not this one," Rafe repeated. "She's got big tits, and she's got the body for it. But otherwise, she's got black hair, and a kinda olive complexion, and she's maybe five-eight. And, boss?"

"Yeah?"

"In my whole life I ain't ever seen a broad like this one."

"What do you mean? She a knockout, or what?"

Rafe's mind was somewhere else. "Huh? Oh, yeah. She's good-lookin', sure. But Vince?" He hesitated briefly. "I hate to say it, but she scares me."

Danelli started to make some other lewd remark, but he saw that his trusted subordinate was serious. "So tell me," he said instead.

"I dunno what it is. I seen her and the others trainin'. She's hell with a blade, and she can shoot the shit outta anythin'."

"So? So she's a good shot. So they all are. What's the big deal? You've seen other guys who're good shots."

Rafe shook his head. "This one's different."

"How?"

"She's stronger than ninety percent of the men in the world. No, make that ninety-five percent."

"So she's strong. Big deal. She a fucking dyke?"

"Huh? Oh, who knows? But that's not the main thing."

"What is the main thing, Rafe?"

"She ain't afraid. I mean, she ain't afraid of nothin', boss. Not killin', not dyin', not anythin'. But the main thing is the killin'."

"What do you mean?"

Rafe recalled what had happened. The weakest of the litter, so to speak, had been executed. He had been allowed to witness it. And she had done it.

With her bare hands.

Just remembering it, Rafe felt a cold lump in the pit of his stomach. It wasn't the death that did it; hell, he'd done worse than that and laughed about it. But this was a broad, a knockout, killing a guy with her bare hands. And liking it.

He started to explain it, to relate the incident to Danelli, and especially the part about the gleam in her eyes. Then, for some strange reason, he thought better of it. So he just shook his head, as though nonplussed.

"She likes it, boss. She likes it a lot. And she's damn good at it."

And so Vinnie had said, what the hell. We've already anted up, anyway, and the pot was "right." He didn't like the idea of a broad in on the caper, unless it involved something to do with sex. But if she was as good as Rafe said she was—and hell, if *he* was afraid of her, she must be—Vinnie would go with it.

So now he had inherited the train caper from Mr. A. Not that he'd had any real choice, of course. And now all the eggs had gone into one basket, that one fucking train.

The New World crazies proved to be as good as Rafe had said they would be. Or at least the few Vince had met, and he had no reason to doubt them when they said the others were just as good.

The airport caper had proved they were good.

It had been Mr. A.'s idea. And, Vince had to grudgingly admit, it had been a good one.

Mr. A. had somehow known the FBI broad would be carrying a copy of a certain report. Supposedly, the report contained everything the Feebs knew about a possible terrorist plot against the train. And by getting the report, Mr. A. would know how much the Feds knew, if anything.

In the dog-eat-dog world of organized crime, Vince Danelli was a survivor. And he had gotten that way by noticing things, and by making good deductions from what he noticed.

It was obvious that Mr. A. must have a snitch in the government somewhere. A leaker, in the Mafia jargon. And the guy had to be highly placed in the government to know about the train.

The leaker wasn't with the Bureau, apparently. That was Danelli's deduction. If he had been a snitch in the Bureau, the boss could have gotten the report directly from him.

So Mr. A. had a leaker high in the government, in a very sensitive position, but not Bureau. That was something for Vinnie to file away for future reference.

Mr. A.'s plan had been designed to get them a copy of whatever the Feds had on them. And it would have given them a chance to test out a couple of the New World crazies in action. To play with their new toy, so to speak.

"Let's wind 'em up and see how they do," the big boss had said to Danelli.

Vince had to admit that the toy had worked well. Damned well. The two gunmen at the airport, both part of the crazies, had mowed down a whole bunch of people, among them the FBI agent.

They had nailed her solid.

She never had a chance. In fact, the whole caper would have come off perfectly if it hadn't been for that guy that Sebastian couldn't remember, the ordinary-looking guy in the tan clothes, the guy who beat Rafe to the briefcase. And iced the two "terrorists" as well.

Vince shook his head grimly.

It had been an expensive test run, he realized, when you thought about Rafe and Hal and Joey and Randy all getting capped. And they didn't even get the report.

However, in terms of testing out their toy, it had gone off well. Nobody—not the cops, the Feds or the press—recognized it as a planned execution of the lady Feebie. They all thought it was just another terrorist attack, and that she just happened to be one of the victims.

That was in many ways the most important part of the test. Officially, the LAX massacre hadn't gone down as a hit at all, let alone a mob hit. And as it turned out, Mr. A. had been able to get his mitts on a copy of the report from another source.

They'd read the report carefully, to find out what the FBI knew about the operation, if anything.

No threat there. The Feds only knew about the train, and about the nuclear material that was going to be on it, and that there might be some vague danger of an unspecified terrorist attempt.

Nothing that mentioned the mob. Nothing that gave any inkling about *their* cargo.

The more Vince thought about it, the more he decided it just might work. And that the New World crazies were just what he needed to make it come off.

Of course, they were a pain in the ass to deal with. The few meetings they had organized to finalize the plan were always supposed to be some big secret deal, always in some foreign country. And dealing with zealots was tiring work. Where in the fuck did Mr. A. come up with these guys? he had wondered, almost as many times as he was now wondering who those bastards were.

But, on balance, it looked as if it just might work, even if the crazies were not the usual type of guys the Mafia used on an operation like this.

But then, there had never been an operation like this.

The plan was simple. And careful.

The crazies would heist the train, this special government project that was hauling some nuclear shit. They would do the dirty work. Get the train stopped. Kill the guards.

Then, when the train was in their hands, the cargo would be split up. Vinnie would see to it that part of the cargo, a special container, went to his organization. And the rest of it would go to the crazies.

They'd make the cargo snatch by helicopter.

Vinnie had been sure to keep things separate. The crazies furnished their choppers, and he furnished one for his people. Then, once the train had been secured, Vinnie's people would swoop down in a big Chinook. It would be specially rigged to hoist the five-ton cargo container.

Rafe was going to be their man on the scene, but Rafe wasn't available any longer. Still, as Vinnie now had it planned, once the actual heist was done, it would be a quick in-and-out operation.

Bring in the chopper. Rappel down a couple of men.

Locate the cargo container they wanted.

Hook up, lift it away, and then haul ass. Leave the crazies to their own heist, taking whatever they wanted of the nuclear shit out by their own choppers.

Let the manhunt that was sure to occur focus on the crazies. And what a shit storm it would be, too, terrorists knocking off a train of H-bomb isotopes. Well, the New World guys were going to take the heat, draw the fire. And if they all got killed, along with a bunch of Feds, or cops, or the fucking U.S. Army, so what? The more the better. By then, Vince's boys would be long gone, their precious cargo airlifted out and concealed, far away from the manhunt and the firefights that would go with it.

It would be the biggest caper ever pulled of.

Vince took another drink of his Scotch. He felt better. He felt a hell of a lot better, in fact.

He wasn't worried about the guys who iced Rafe and Joey and Randy and Hal. They weren't cops, and they weren't Feds. Good as they were, the New World crazies were just as good, or better. And there were more of the crazies.

Hell, let 'em shoot the shit outta each other, he thought.

He just wished he could be there to see it.

On second thought, maybe he would be. With Rafe gone, the operation didn't have a field commander. Maybe he'd go on location himself.

Might be kinda fun, at that.

14

Brognola had arranged for military rather than commercial transportation for the team to the West Coast. It simply meant placing a call to a certain party in Washington, D.C. This party was about the highest human power alive, and because the Lambda operation was being conducted under his personal authority, things got done.

The team got to San Diego by a Navy jet that took them to Miramar Naval Air Station. NAS Miramar, made famous by the movie *Top Gun*, was located only a few miles directly north of downtown San Diego. From there, a helicopter transported them—and their luggage—directly to the Marine Corps Recruit Depot, MCRD.

When Able Team arrived at MCRD, a driver was waiting to take them to the train.

He was a squared-away Marine, and he asked no questions. In fact, he looked as if transporting three civilians in green jump suits from a special chopper to a railroad siding was the most natural thing in the world, never mind that it didn't take much imagination to conclude that their bags contained mainly weaponry.

No questions asked, and no information volunteered.

When they arrived at the compound, he unloaded their gear with practiced efficiency. Then he turned to face them.

"Will there be anything else, sir?" he asked. It was not clear to which of them the question was addressed.

"No," Lyons said simply.

"Sir, thank you, sir." Not knowing who these crazy civilians might be, or their rank, and figuring it was best to cover all bases, he clicked his heels and snapped off a salute. Lyons acknowledged it with a distracted nod of his head, and the driver got back in the van and departed.

The ground transport had again been arranged by, or thanks to the clout of, Brognola.

It wasn't that the team lacked the time to use commercial flights or local taxis. In fact, there would have been ample time for both. However, the security folks at Delta or TWA or United just might have been a little concerned about what was inside the luggage the three men carried with them.

The Stony Man chief had anticipated such a problem. Besides, he wanted to give the team an extra day at Stony Man Farm to get outfitted, and discuss strategies.

And, incidentally, to rest up.

It had occurred to Brognola that he was sending his team in under substantially less than optimal conditions. The exigencies of war often required that, but he still didn't like it. The odds were long enough anyway; why make them even longer by going in with two-thirds of the force operating at less than one hundred percent?

Yet that was what had to be.

To begin with, Lyons had just suffered an emotional blow of staggering proportions, Julie's death. And, though he seemed to be taking it as much in stride as circumstances permitted, Brognola had a lingering concern that it would affect his efficiency. If nothing else, it had to affect his eating and sleeping, to say nothing of his alertness.

And Gadgets was still feeling the effects of the trauma to his shoulder and rib cage. The injury had been the result of hitting the windshield when he tried to jump up to avoid the onrushing Lincoln Continental, whose driver had wanted the Able Team commando to be the filling between a two-car sandwich.

At the time, a combination of daze and adrenaline had kept him from feeling much. But as the hours passed, that had changed.

It had hurt like the devil when he breathed deeply, and it hurt just as badly to raise his left arm in a certain way. But that was no big deal. Gadgets, perhaps even more than the other two men, could mentally block out pain.

The real cause for concern lay elsewhere.

When he had awakened for the meeting at Stony Man Farm on the morning after the incident, Gadgets had felt pain that was different from the bruises. It was a sharp, pinched feeling, and it ran from the middle of his back up the left side of his neck. Occasionally, too, he felt it shoot down his left arm.

"Pinched nerve in your spine, maybe," said Blancanales. The former Black Beret had received basic medical training while in the military. "If it gets worse, it could be serious."

Over Gadgets's protests, Brognola had ordered a medical examination to be performed on his ace fighter.

"Fuck that," was the latter's response. "Sir," he added hastily.

Like most fighting men—along with serious athletes and a lot of ordinary folk, as well—Gadgets believed doctors usually meant bad news.

Common sense told him, of course, that the physician didn't actually create the injury, but instead merely reported what was already there. Still, his mind didn't like to accept that. As a result, the medical personnel found themselves in the position of being the messengers who brought the bad news.

"If a doctor hasn't said it's a problem, I can pretend it isn't a problem," ran the mental logic. Until a doctor diagnosed it, it didn't really exist.

In ancient times, messengers who brought bad news were sometimes executed. And with the doctor being the messenger with the possible bad news, Gadgets was entertaining some feelings that that system should be reinstated.

Brognola, who understood that analysis, wasn't having any of it. Moreover, he seemed edgier and more irritable than the three men had ever remembered seeing him. The medical exam would, repeat, would be conducted, he ruled. No further argument, no appeal.

"Look, Chief," Gadgets had argued anyway, "I don't need a doctor."

"That's fine, but I want a doctor to tell me that. You're about to put your ass on the line, and I want to know you're healthy before you do it."

"It's my ass," Gadgets observed.

"And also theirs." Brognola gestured vaguely at Blancanales and Lyons. "Not to mention the mission's. All I want is to be sure you're in good shape to do this."

Blancanales, who had been standing by, murmured, "Better to be a healthy corpse than an injured one, I guess."

Brognola turned sharply around. "What did you say?" he'd snapped.

"Uh, nothing, Chief."

Gadgets took up the argument again. "I can already tell you what it is, Chief. A doctor won't do anything that I can't already take care of myself."

Brognola's voice was heavy with sarcasm. "Oh? And tell me, Herr Dr. Schwarz, what medical college you attended? Or was this a home-study course? Surgery Made Simple? Something like that?"

"I know it's nothing but a hell of a deep bruise," Gadgets had persisted. "Maybe a little pinched nerve, but mainly just a fucking bruise."

"Oh? And is that the medical term for it?"

"I don't know the medical term. A 'bone bruise,' as we used to call them when I was a kid. It's just gonna hurt like hell until it heals, that's all."

"And when I hear it from a doctor, I'll believe it," rejoined the chief. "Now get moving. That's an order."

The physician was an orthopedic surgeon named Bron. He was a large, heavy-set man with a sour expression and unusually small, agile hands. The flesh of his face was permanently molded into a configuration that suggested he had just gargled with vinegar.

Dr. Bron began the examination by using those hands to poke and prod all around Gadgets's neck, shoulder, and upper spine. It seemed as if he sought to gauge the extent of the injury by the amount of pain the prodding produced. Then he ordered Gadgets to move his arm in a circle, rotate his head on his neck, and generally tested out the moving parts in that area of his body. Finally, he ordered a full set of X rays.

He pinned the X rays up against a bright, translucent screen and examined them.

"Hmmm," he said thoughtfully.

A pang of fear hit Gadgets. What if something were really injured? Something that did more than hurt, that could incapacitate him? Visions of dreadful injury danced before him, some kind of swelling that caused pressure to a main nerve or even the spinal cord, and an insidious, creeping paralysis....

He tried to console himself by the knowledge that, irritable or not, Brognola couldn't scrub the mission. The train had to go through, and the chief wanted them on it. You couldn't just reschedule a terrorist hijacking, he thought.

Something about that thought stirred at the back of his consciousness, but he put it aside for the time being.

The more immediate thing that disturbed him was how to get by this examination and get a clean bill of health for the mission. Dr. Bron, he felt sure, was not the type who could be bribed, threatened or cajoled into altering the record of his diagnosis.

Then he had an idea. Maybe he could just, uh, "underreport" the true findings to Brognola. It wouldn't be a lie, exactly, just a loose interpretation of the facts.

Almost immediately, however, he realized it wouldn't work. Dr. Bron, he knew, was not his own doctor, but was Brognola's. It was just like the military or the NFL. And Gadgets felt sure the medico would report his findings directly to the chief.

That left only one way out, assuming the report was bad.

He would have to convince Brognola to let him do the mission despite whatever injury he was found to have. As long as the other guys were willing—and as long as it didn't materially increase the risk to them—what the hell?

Gadgets knew he could withstand pain as well as any human alive. He'd done it before. And he was willing to do it again to go on this mission. The only consideration was whether something would give out on him at a crucial time, so as to endanger the others or jeopardize the operation.

He decided he simply wouldn't let that happen.

Mind over matter, and all that stuff. Just work through the pain. Hell, it wouldn't be the first time somebody had overcome pain and injury simply by the brass on his balls. Hadn't the famed test pilot, Chuck Yeager, been injured with a shoulder separation when he made the historic flight that broke the sound barrier?

Besides, Blancanales had a good point. In the final analysis, it might well come down to nothing more than the difference between a previously injured corpse and a healthy one.

Dr. Bron continued to study the X rays. He peered at one and then the other. Then he pursed his lips and shook his head.

"What is it?" inquired Gadgets.

"Hard to tell."

Bastard, thought Gadgets. Don't play games with me, asshole. You're the fucking doctor. You're supposed to be able to tell. Aloud he politely inquired, "What's your best medical opinion, then?"

"Closest I can say is that you've probably got a hell of a deep bruise."

Gadgets couldn't believe his ears. If you're fucking with me, doctor, he thought, I'll rip off your sour face. "That's it?" he demanded.

"It's sometimes called a bone bruise," Dr. Bron added, "but that's something of a misnomer, actually."

"So what's the bottom line, Doc? Is it going to affect me in this mission?"

The doctor shrugged. "Probably just hurt like hell until it heals, that's all."

"Question, Doctor," said Gadgets after a moment.

"Yes?"

"Could you do me a favor?"

"What is it?"

"Put it in writing for the chief? The way you said it just now? I mean, in *exactly* those terms?"

And so Brognola had eaten a little crow. It was just a little, but to Gadgets that was better than none at all. And Brognola shrugged and realized that whether his guys were a hundred percent or not, they would have to do.

Besides, they did have brass balls. And, in the final analysis, that was what made the difference between winning and losing. Or living and dying.

Attitude, in other words.

15

The train turned out to be a total of nine units, seven cars plus two diesel locomotives. It was a particularly unspectacular assembly of plain-looking cars. In a word, it was nondescript.

"I suppose," Gadgets observed facetiously, "they could have painted the whole thing bright yellow, with nuclear symbols plastered all over it. And maybe a sign, Keep Clear, Hydrogen Bomb in Transit."

"Or maybe skull-and-crossbone warnings all over it," agreed the Politician.

Tired as he was, Lyons forced a grin in acknowledgment of the kidding. "Or put little mushroom clouds all over it," he suggested. "And Nuke Jane Fonda bumper stickers."

The train began and ended with a diesel locomotive. In between were the seven cars.

"Only two of them are hot," Gadgets pointed out.

"What are the rest of them for?"

"Who knows? My guess is that we'll be in one of them, one of those two passenger cars." He pointed to the two rail cars.

"And the others?"

Gadgets shrugged. "Probably fillers. Empties thrown in so it doesn't look too obvious, the way it would if it was just a couple of engines and three cars on a cross-country run."

Next to the front locomotive and the passenger car, the next two cars carried the nuclear materials. After that came two flatcars with huge containerized cargo boxes on them. The next car was an empty flat car, while the last one before the rear locomotive was another passenger car.

Blancanales pointed to one of the containerized cargo boxes. "What do you figure that is?"

Gadgets wrinkled his brow. "I don't know. It isn't listed on the manifest."

"Manifest?" Lyons asked. "What manifest? This is a ghost train, remember?"

"I mean," Gadgets attempted to respond, "the report the chief gave—"

Lyons interrupted him. "While you're checking the manifest, Homes, tell me what the stuff in the other two cars, the hot cars, is listed as. Wild rice? Dope? Condoms?"

"All right, all right. So I can't talk." A chagrined Gadgets continued to check the report. "Not listed here," he announced finally.

Lyons shrugged. "Hell, who cares? We got the room, so what does it matter?"

"Probably doesn't," Gadgets agreed. "Unless it's a bomb or something," he added with a grin.

"Somehow," Lyons mused aloud, "I had the impression it would be longer than this."

Gadgets allowed a wry smile. "I guess in terms of size, or bulk, the stuff it takes to make H-bombs doesn't take up too much room."

"I thought they measured H-bombs in terms of tons of TNT."

"That's different. They're saying the explosion equaled the explosion of a certain amount of TNT. But that's a calibration only, and it relates to the blast, not the physical size of the bomb."

"Oh."

"Remember, actually all they're doing is splitting and combining atoms. And this train isn't hauling completed bombs, only the raw material, the isotopes, to make them."

"Thanks, Professor."

"There'll be a test at the end of the hour."

"Open book? Multiple choice?"

"Well, open minds. And, as a professor I once had in a physics class said, 'Every test is multiple choice—it's just that the choices won't be given to you.'"

"Guy was a real comedian," observed Lyons sarcastically, "a laugh-a-minute."

The Politician joined in with a grin. "Hard to make physics too humorous, I guess."

Gadgets was frowning thoughtfully. "Or," he mused, "if you want to get metaphysical about it, you could say that all the choices are given to you. They exist in the universe. It's just up to you to find them, that's all." He spoke as if he hadn't heard Lyons's comment, but at the end of his statement gave a wink to show he was kidding.

Lyons looked at his partner as if he'd lost his mind. "Like I said," the Ironman commented at last in an attempt to get back to matters at hand, "I thought it would be longer."

"That's what *she* said," quipped Blancanales. "But then," he added with exaggerated false modesty, "I showed the rest of it, and...well, any concerns in that area vanished." He made a gesture with his hands. "Poof!"

"I just hope," Lyons observed to nobody in particular, "that you guys fight as well as you bullshit."

They walked toward the ghost train.

The nine rail vehicles sat on a siding near the Marine Corps Recruit Depot, or MCRD, in San Diego. No guards were visible. The only apparent security was that the siding itself was inside a fenced compound, and the three men had to be cleared by a sentry at the gate before they could enter.

The theory, Brognola had explained earlier, was that secrecy and anonymity were used to protect the train, instead of making it an obvious military transport. In fact, there would only be eight persons aboard—two people to run the train, three scientists or technicians, both civilians, to monitor the level of radioactivity in case of an unexpected leak or other difficulty, and the three men of Able Team.

"Question, Chief," Lyons had asked during one of the follow-up briefing sessions at Stony Man Farm the preceding day.

"Shoot."

"Do the five civilians know what's up?"

Brognola hesitated. "What do you mean?"

"I mean the engineers and the scientists. Do they know they'll be riding into an ambush? Are they volunteers?"

The face of the Stony Man Chief of Operations became expressionless. "No to both."

"Will they be told who we are?"

Brognola hesitated. "No," he said at last. "Not by me, anyway."

Gadgets arched an eyebrow and frowned. Blancanales remained expressionless. Lyons fixed the head of Stony Man operations with a cold gaze. "One final question on this area."

"Yes?"

"Do they have any combat training?"

Brognola shook his head. "Negative."

"None?"

"None. I've reviewed their personnel jackets. Those files are, as you might imagine, quite extensive due to the highly sensitive nature of the job. No military backgrounds. No ex-cops. None of them even takes karate on his own time at a storefront dojo, if that's the right term. A couple of them jog, but that's it. They are peaceful civilians. Period."

Lyons thought that over. Finally, he said, "Sorry to be blunt about this, Chief, but I take it that whoever is running this mission considers those persons expendable?"

A look of fatigue, and maybe even a touch of sadness, came over Brognola. "There are a lot of variables working here. This is one aspect of a bigger operation. One important engagement in a bigger theater of war, so to speak."

He hesitated and then went on. It was apparent to the others that he was choosing his words with extraordinary care.

"In answer to your question, yes. They are, in a sense, expendable."

Lyons nodded grimly. "Just as long as we know the rules, Chief."

"It is hoped," Brognola had continued, "that no innocent lives will be lost. But let me make one thing clear. In terms of your mission, stopping the hijacking and killing the terrorists is your number-one priority. Your only priority, in fact.

"Trust no one. Warn no one. Confide in no one.

"When the attack comes—if it comes—shoot your way clear as best you can. Kill as many of the terrorists as you can."

Lyons's thoughts returned to the present and the mission before Able Team. The Ironman checked the massive stainless-steel Rolex on his left wrist. "Sixty minutes to lift-off."

The other two nodded without comment, and the three men boarded the train.

16

The two passenger cars, almost identical on the outside, proved to be very different inside.

The front portion of the first one Able Team examined, which was just in front of the rear locomotive, was fitted with comfortable bench seats. In that respect, it resembled an ordinary Amtrak passenger car. In the rear one-third of the car, however, the seats had been removed, and work tables had been fitted in their place.

The work tables contained a variety of electronic, radio and computer gear.

"What's that?" Lyons asked, pointing at it. His voice was curt, almost surly.

Gadgets glanced first at his partner, and then at the tables. He ran a practised eye over the equipment, then made his report. "Looks like communications, a security system for the hot cars, and monitors to detect any problem with the cargo."

"Great," was Lyons's moody reply.

They made their way to the other passenger car, behind the front locomotive. It proved to be a combination Pullman and galley. The sleeping rooms with their berths were at the front of the car, while the kitchen and tables took up the back portion.

Lyons made his way down the narrow passage and pushed open the door to one of the rooms. Then he maneuvered his bags inside it and put them on the floor. Gadgets and Blancanales entered the room after him, though they did not bring their gear.

They watched as Lyons crossed the small room to the window. He muttered something unintelligible, then gazed outside with his forearm against the window frame.

"Ironman." It was Blancanales's voice. "Amigo. What's eating you?"

Lyons looked at him. "What makes you think anything is eating me?"

"Amigo."

"What?"

"This is me. The Politician. Your buddy. I know you. Now you've had your head up your ass all day. I know it, and you know it. What's up? Is it just about Julie? Or is there something else?"

For several long moments, Lyons regarded his partner with a cold stare. Perhaps for the first time since they had known each other, Blancanales found himself wondering if he could take Lyons. If they really went to fist city, who would come out the winner?

Lyons was, of course, bigger and heavier. Not as much these days as before, light as the Ironman was. Blancanales, on the other hand, had more combat experience than Lyons. Moreover, the former Black Beret had been trained in a variety of unarmed combat methods.

Virtually all of them were lethal.

Lyons was stronger. And he had a capacity for combat that was truly awe-inspiring. A will to survive, to win, to kill. Pain fueled him with greater determination. The heavier the odds against him, the more psycho he became.

Scary, actually.

Blancanales was better trained in both the mental and physical aspects of fighting, and killing. And, though he did not have the raw physical power that Lyons had, the Politician was in his own right tremendously strong, with a lean, tight musculature that packed his stocky frame. And he had a mental discipline that did not know fear.

One was very strong, well disciplined and trained to an incredibly high degree.

The other was only well trained, but incredibly strong, and possessed of almost psychotic mental resiliency.

Who would win?

The two men looked at each other. Lyons's eyes were a bleak, icy gray-blue, with the endless coldness of a barren glacier. Blancanales's dark brown eyes glittered almost black, shiny spots of flint-hard obsidian.

Nobody spoke for a full thirty seconds.

Then, at last, Lyons broke the spell. "Aw, fuck, I don't know, partner. I know I've had my head up my ass. And for the life of me, I don't know why."

"Julie?" said the Politician softly.

Lyons shook his head distractedly. "No, not really. I mean, that's part of it, sure. But it's something about this whole goddamn thing."

"What?"

"That's just it. I don't know. I just can't put my finger on it. But it doesn't add up."

"What doesn't?"

"This mission. Somebody's holding back. But I can't say or see why."

Gadgets spoke for the first time. "Yeah, Ironman, I know what you mean. It's been bothering me, too." As he spoke, he recalled the thought that had been nibbling at his mind when he was in the doctor's office.

After a few moments, Lyons spoke again. "The chief said that he believed the Russians didn't necessarily think these NWI assholes could really pull this off, right?"

Gadgets nodded. "Their mission is to just make a hell of a good try at it. That would cause the media and Congressional shit storm they were after. And if they got it, so much the better."

Lyons nodded. Then the cop in him went to work.

Assuming the chief was right about the Soviets' mission, he thought, it raised a hell of a question about Able Team's mission.

Why, he thought, was Able Team being called in? Why not just load the train with a thousand Special Forces types, and let them shoot the shit out of any would-be hijackers?

Hell, if the government knew this much about the NWI plans, just substitute rocks for the real H-bomb stuff, let the raid take place, then arrest them all and call it another successful FBI "sting" operation. That way, the U.S. couldn't lose.

But they weren't doing that.

No, there had to be more to it. Just as the Russians were using NWI to do their dirty work, so somebody in the U.S. government was using Able Team.

Well, he amended hastily, not that we're doing anybody's dirty work in exactly the same way NWI is—after all, we're only defending our country against an act of aggression. Still and all, there were some similarities, maybe more than he liked to admit existed....

Finally he spoke. "What's the big picture, do you think?" he asked speculatively.

"What do you mean, amigo?" the Politician responded.

"What are we really trying to protect? What exactly are we trying to do here?"

"Stop the terrorists from taking over the Lambda shipment. That's what the chief said."

Lyons shook his head. "No, we're not," he asserted bluntly.

"Why do you say that, Homes?" asked Gadgets.

The Ironman explained his theory. "So," he concluded, "if I really just wanted to prevent the hijacking, I'd just load this train with five hundred Special Forces guys and let them shoot the shit out of anything that moved."

"Or just cancel the train run," said Gadgets. "Do it later, if you're so worried."

"Or cover it from the air," put in the Politician. "Hell, call in an air strike the moment the terrorists hit. You're right, amigo. There's got to be more to this than what we've been told."

Lyons nodded. "Not that it's such a big deal that we don't know the big picture, of course. Goes with the territory that you just trust the leaders, and go do your thing."

"But..." Gadgets said inquiringly.

"But the risk is that we'll piss in somebody's carrot patch," Lyons said crudely, "when we could just as easily have pissed the other way, only we didn't know the carrot patch was there."

"On the other hand," said Gadgets, "if the Chief's not worried about that, why should we be? Hell, he knows what he's doing. If he didn't tell us, it was because he had a good reason not to."

"If we knew, it might save our asses," responded Lyons. "That's why. By knowing what the enemy knows, by knowing what this mission is all about, we stand a better chance of survival."

"Or of spilling our guts if we get caught and squeezed," said Gadgets pointedly.

Lyons ignored him. The mists were beginning to break, the light beginning to dawn. A faint smile traced his lips, and he nodded his head slowly.

"And I think I have a pretty good idea of what this is all about," the Ironman said at last.

17

Blancanales and Gadgets looked at their partner.

Lyons nodded, more to himself than to them. "There's a leak," he declared. "There's a fucking leak."

"What do you mean, amigo?"

"There's a leak, man. *That's* why we're here."

"I think I follow you, Homes," said Gadgets. "Partway, at least. Go ahead."

"We're here as decoys to find the leak. That's what's at stake, not just a bunch of H-bomb ingredients."

The other two looked at him, and waited.

"Look at the facts. One, the CIA or whoever put Brognola up to this knows about the hijacking.

"They know it's going to happen, and who is doing it, and even what train it'll be. Now, how do they know that?"

"An informant, Homes? A source, as the Feebies say?" asked Gadgets.

Lyons nodded. "Got to be. They've got a snitch into the terrorists. That's why they can't just cancel the train. The terrorists would suspect something. Start looking for the informer. And maybe figure out who he is."

"Or she," said Gadgets speculatively.

"Or she."

"Okay," said the Politician. "I can buy that, amigo. But it still doesn't explain why they don't load this bastard up with Green Berets and have air cover."

"I know. And I think the reason is that the chief suspects the leak goes both ways.

"I think there must have been a breach of security on our side as well. To put it bluntly, there's a traitor someplace, and the chief is trying to flush him out."

A slow grin spread over Gadgets's face. "A spy. A fucking mole," he said.

The Ironman nodded eagerly. "It's got to be. It's the only explanation that fits."

"Where do you think he's placed?" inquired the Able Team wizard.

Lyons shook his head. "I can't say. Probably not Bureau, and certainly not anybody close to Stony Man. My guess is somebody in the Nuclear Regulatory Commission, or the Department of Defense, maybe."

"A mole," Gadgets repeated softly.

The more Lyons thought about it, the clearer it became. As he spoke, the facts looked more convincing than ever. "That's why they couldn't have any elaborate plans, anything that would attract attention. Hell, the chief as much as said he was working just for the President on this one. I'll bet the rest of the people involved in the Lambda train don't even know we're here."

"The civilians," Gadgets said, as if that confirmed what Lyons had just said.

"What about them?" inquired Blancanales.

"The chief told us the civilians were expendable. Remember what he said about our priorities? How he 'hoped' nobody got hurt, but if they did—"

"If they did, tough shit," Lyons cut in.

Blancanales nodded. "I remember. It surprised me a little," he said softly. "And I don't think he liked saying it, either, amigos. I don't think he liked it at all."

"I agree."

Gadgets made a John Wayne imitation. "A man's gotta do what a man's gotta do."

Lyons gave a nod of agreement, though his expression was serious. "He's a ruthless bastard when he has to be. Including with us. Our lives are expendable. Hell, we all know that, and we agreed to it by signing on. But I don't think he liked applying those rules to the civilians. He just didn't have any choice. If he tried to make any other arrangement—say, switch some volunteers for the civilians, anything like that—"

"It would have alerted the mole," Blancanales said at last.

Gadgets frowned thoughtfully. "It makes sense, I guess. Something had been bothering me, too. And this feels like the answer."

"One thing I don't understand," said Blancanales.

"What?"

"Say you're right about the mole. How is this going to help find him?"

Lyons shrugged. "It might not. But it will save the nuclear stuff. It'll also give us a shot at the terrorists, the chance to nail a lot of them without giving away the informant. None of that could have happened if any major change of plans had gone down. The mole might have been alerted, and then we wouldn't even have that much."

"But this way will ultimately reveal the informant with the NWI, amigo," the Politician pointed out. "They'll figure it out when the hijackers run into us."

"Maybe," Lyons agreed. "And maybe not."

"Or," Gadgets observed, "Maybe the chief is telling the CIA to pull the informant out right when the hijacking is attempted, and before they can get back to kill him."

"What about the mole?"

Gadgets grinned. "I don't know, but my guess is that Kurtzman is working on that."

It was Lyons's turn to look surprised. "Why do you say that?"

"Well, if I were the chief, and I had this little surprise—us—in store for the New World creeps, I'd be figuring that once the hijacking went to shit, the mole would have some explaining to do."

"They'll make contact with him, you mean, after this goes down," Lyons agreed.

"Exactly. And, even though you don't know who he is, you probably have it narrowed down to a few suspects."

"Hell, there can't be more than a few possibilities anyway," Lyons agreed.

"Right. And if I were the chief, I'd have electronic surveillance and phone taps and every other big-brother device in the world going on the main suspects. So that after the hijacking fails, if any suspicious contact is made, he'll be able to know who gets called on the carpet. Pinpoint the mole, in other words."

"And Kurtzman?" inquired Lyons. "Why did you say him?"

"Well, there's nobody better."

"That's true."

"And besides, when I called the Farm from that gas station after the LAX massacre, somebody else answered the phone. When the chief came on the line, and I asked where Kurtzman was, he said he was busy on something else. 'I've got Kurtzman doing other things,' I think he said."

For the first time, Lyons grinned a real grin. "Very good, pal. It fits. That's got to be it."

After a moment, Gadgets said, "So, Ironman. Now that you've figured it out, where does it leave us? What good does it do us to know?"

Lyons grinned again. "Maybe none. But I feel better, at least."

"There is that," Gadgets agreed.

"And now," the Ironman continued, "if I could only figure out what that 'Axis Powers' bullshit means."

Blancanales suddenly glanced out the window. "Well, you'll have to hold on to that, Ironman. Here come our civilians."

The civilians were five in number, just as Brognola had said.

Two were "diesel drivers," as Gadgets referred to them. Their names were Herbert Brown and Chuck White.

"Brown and White," repeated Blancanales with his easy politician's grin that negated any possible hint of offensiveness. "Should be easy enough to remember."

Both men were dark, heavy-set men in their forties. They had the leathery faces and the stocky sturdiness of workingmen who had spent a lifetime in the outdoors. As far as they knew, this was just another train ride, one more easy, cross-country run. No questions asked, no answers given.

They nodded their greeting at the three men in dark-green jump suits, three more crazy civilians going from west to east with the train.

Lyons looked at the other government people who had boarded the train, the scientist and technician types who would be monitoring the train's precious cargo.

One was an owlish scientist of about forty named Tom Haley. He was balding and dumpy with thinning brown hair and thick glasses and a perpetually worried look on his face. Tommy the Owl, Lyons thought.

The second, named Mike Swann, had the rangy, athletic look of a tennis pro. On a closer inspection,

Lyons revised that initial impression, and made Swann to be an engineer, probably a few years out of college. He was a young professional in government service. Swann had light brown hair, stylishly short, and a neatly trimmed mustache.

Swann's arms and face sported a nice tan, Lyons noted, but it didn't look like the kind of tan he'd earned on the beach playing volleyball, or at the country club, even. It was too smooth and even. If he had gotten it at a country club, it was under sunlamps and not on the tennis courts. And his body, though not fat, looked soft.

Lyons recalled that Brognola had said that none of the civilians had any combat training. And this guy was living proof of that.

Lyons decided that he didn't care much for Swann. The young engineer had something of the spoiled pretty-boy about him, a sort of petulance that Lyons thought unmanly.

It was also obvious that pretty-boy Swann had definite designs on the third member of their group, a young woman named Beverly Becker.

Lyons could understand the designs. And, in a slick, glossy sort of way, he saw that Beverly and Swann would make a good couple, she of the clean, olive complexion and dark exotic good looks, and he the tanned, country-club golden boy.

She was about five-eight or -nine, Lyons estimated. Well, maybe five-eight, but she looked taller. She had a certain presence about her, enhanced by her open confidence and grace.

His practiced cop's eye took inventory, then moved on. She, on the other hand, met his gaze frankly and kept her eyes focused on the Able Team warrior.

"Hi," she said, extending her hand to Lyons and then turning to the others after the introductions had been made. "I'm the new girl."

Her smile was magnetic, her teeth flashing white against her complexion.

Lyons was not impressed. Though she was beautiful, with a body that would jump start a five-thousand-year-old mummy, something about her seemed phony.

She sure was in shape, though, he noted. And her hand was hard and strong, with a toughness to the edge adjacent to her little finger that bespoke some martial art, karate perhaps.

All in all, a pretty impressive package. And probably a passion engine in the sack, too, all hot flesh and jutting breasts....

And she left him utterly cold.

He remembered another woman with dark hair and vital good looks who had not been phony. Of course, the comparison wasn't fair; most women looked shallow next to that woman.

Only she was dead. Dust to dust. And maybe the pain of that memory, that recent loss was what made this woman seem artificial to him.

"Hi," he said shortly, then turned away.

Lyons wondered if he would ever snap out of it. Right now, he didn't really care much if he lived or died, except that he had a score to settle with the people who had killed his woman. The euphoria he had felt at figuring out what was going on with the case was gone, and in its place was a deadly listlessness.

And the presence of this dark, exotic beauty just made it worse.

She meant nothing to him personally, except as one of the civilians who were considered expendable. Maybe, he reflected, that was what bothered him, that another beautiful woman would likely die in a firefight with terrorist assholes.

What the hell, he thought. Everybody had to go sometime.

Yeah, but I volunteered. So did Gadgets and Pol. And so did Julie, even.

What about the others? Brown and White. And a dumpy scientist named Tommy the Owl, who probably had a devoted dumpy little wife and a couple of dumpy kids who loved him. And even pretty-boy Swann, and a dark, exotic beauty who looked like a cross between a model and a jock.

Just because they weren't his type didn't mean they should die. Pretty-boys and somehow artificial model types had a right to live, too.

Idly, he wondered how she had gotten that faint scar along her jaw.

18

Lyons for once had half expected the trip to be a special straight-through express, with tracks and routes cleared to let them shoot through. In fact, it had turned out to be anything but that.

As Brognola had said, secrecy was the key. And secrecy meant a low-profile journey, punctuated by spells of stopping and waiting for clearances to be arranged and gaps in the ordinary railway traffic to occur.

Their route had taken them to Chicago, and would then lead them generally south and east to Oak Ridge. As Gadgets put it with a faint smile, "I guess every self-respecting train has to go through Chicago."

"How so?" Lyons asked.

"It's the railway hub of the whole country."

"Oh."

"At least we should be fairly safe here."

"Why so?"

"Look around you. It isn't likely they'll attempt to hijack it in the middle of one of the biggest cities in the country. Nobody in his right mind would do it here, when there are a million better places along the way."

"Yeah, I guess not."

"Get some sleep, Ironman."

"Yeah. I guess so."

It was after midnight when their short train slowed to a halt, accompanied by the long squeals of metal and the occasional explosive *huff* of compressed air that operated brakes and other types of mechanical apparatus.

Nothing moved.

The switchyard was deserted, or at least the part where the train had come to a stop. Far away, the heavy metallic clangs and clanks of industry cut the night air. A dense, cold fog descended over the area. It muffled the sounds and diffused the distant yellow lights, adding to the desolation. The faint, foul chemical smell of sulfur permeated the air.

It was a scene from an industrial hell, Lyons thought, a dark wasteland of steel rails and stained wooden ties and the sharp rectangular hulks of railroad cars.

He sniffed the acrid, rotten-egg odor.

"Jesus," he muttered, "we've got the brimstone; now all we need is the fire."

In the distance, train whistles hooted. Diesel locomotives roared and whined, and from somewhere, far away, came the heavy throb of an engine, probably a turbine of some sort.

Blancanales had the watch, but Lyons was unable to sleep.

Logic told him Gadgets was right in his earlier comment, that nobody in his right mind would try an assault there. But something in his gut said, don't be too sure. So he lay there, fully clad, his eyes open and his mind roaming.

Maybe "in his right mind" was the key, he thought idly. The New World Insurrectionists *weren't* in their right minds. He shut his eyes and tried to doze.

Suddenly, out of the background noises, his acute hearing focused on one. It was gradually becoming more prominent than the others, and with a start he realized it was the turbine he had heard earlier.

A helicopter.

No, make that two, no, three helicopters.

Instantly, he rolled to his feet. There could be any number of innocent choppers—police, news or flying ambulances. For some reason, though, he didn't think so.

He reached for the weapons that lay near him. One was a Colt Python, the same type of firearm he had favored in his early years as a cop. It had a six-inch barrel, topped with a ventilated rib that ran the length of it. The Python, or its Smith & Wesson counterpart, the Model 19, had been his mainstay sidearm in those days.

Later, he had been persuaded that in many respects—especially for close-quarter combat—the .45 Government Model Colt semiauto was a superior weapon. And he had reluctantly agreed that it made sense for all three men to carry the same weapon, so the ammo would be interchangeable.

But for this mission he carried the Python.

It was a sort of psychological thing for him, he supposed. Ballistics be damned, he *wanted* to carry the revolver. And the confidence he felt with it made up for the other gun's possible superiority.

And if it didn't, tough.

The other weapon was the Atchisson shotgun, a sleek, assault-rifle look-alike in 12 gauge. This particular gun had been modified to fire full-auto as well as semiauto. It had a unique feature custom-installed by the Stony Man weaponsmith, Cowboy Kissinger—the ability to fire three-shot full-auto bursts.

Without jamming.

Lyons liked the three-shot blasts.

The gun jumped in his hands like the kick of a mule when he fired it in that mode. It was essentially a barely controlled explosion, a blast that threatened to jerk the weapon right out of his grip. Loaded with double-ought buck—twelve pellets per magnum round—or two rounds of double-ought with a single, ounce-sized slug round between them, the three-shot blast would knock down a horse. And chew it to pieces.

Grabbing the Atchisson, Lyons padded softly toward the rear of the car.

Blancanales and Gadgets were already moving. Their combat-trained ears had detected the choppers even before Lyons.

"Indians!" hissed the former.

"Let's get clear of the train before they land!" snapped Lyons. "Move it!"

The fog-muffled throbbing of the helicopter engines grew closer. The three men hurried to the door. Suddenly, a shadowy figure confronted them. Then a light came on, and the figure wasn't shadowy any longer.

Beverly!

"What is it?" she asked. Her eyes looked wide and frightened. "What's going on? What are all those guns for?"

"Nothing," Lyons snapped. Jesus, he thought, the little twit's scared! One of the "expendable" civilians. He didn't like to think about it; Julie's death was still too fresh in his mind. Pretty women weren't supposed to die like that.

"No, it's not nothing," she persisted. "What are you going to do?"

"You just stay inside while we go check."

"Who are you?" Beverly demanded, a tremble in her voice that sounded near to panic. "I thought you were just workmen, here to take care of the cargo."

"We're workmen, all right," Lyons muttered, pushing by her. "And now we gotta go to work."

The three men dropped off the train to the ground. The roar of the turbine engines increased until it was deafening.

Suddenly a chopper running without lights was right overhead. The men felt the powerful down-blast of the prop wash. Then the massive, ungainly machine was touching down some thirty or forty yards away from the train. Armed soldiers swarmed out, spooky shapes in the eddying mist.

There was no mistaking their intention.

"Scatter out!" Lyons hissed.

The three men crouched and ran, Gadgets and Blancanales toward the end of the train, Lyons toward the front.

Suddenly, one of the soldiers shouted something. It was in a language that Lyons didn't immediately recognize. And, although the figures were still enshrouded in fog, the Able Team men understood—or thought they understood—that they had been spotted.

"We're burned!" said the Politician in a low urgent voice over his shoulder to the retreating form of Lyons.

"Now!" the Ironman yelled in response.

As one, the three men made a quarter-turn so that they were facing the commandos coming off the helicopter. As one they opened fire.

Blancanales and Gadgets—figuring that if Lyons could do it, they could do it as well—carried weapons of their own choosing, and standardization be damned.

The former had an M-16, the workhorse assault rifle of Vietnam, with full-auto and semiauto selector switch. In 5.56 mm, with a 30-round clip-type magazine, it was the same weapon Blancanales had used in Vietnam, though for some of his Special Forces missions he had used a shortened version.

Selector on autoburn, he crouched slightly and began raking the figures with fierce fire.

Gadgets carried an Uzi submachine gun, the 9 mm Israeli-developed assault carbine.

Though he, too, had carried the M-16 in Vietnam, Gadgets was by nature more of an experimenter than Blancanales. He also had a streak of the nonconformist in him, and partly for that reason he favored the Israeli weapon for close-quarter work of the type he'd anticipated he'd encounter on this mission.

Sort of like a machete or sword as opposed to a bow and arrow.

He knew, of course, that the M-16's 5.56 mm round was vastly superior to the Uzi's 9 mm in terms of muzzle velocity, foot-pounds of energy and range. And in most open terrain firefights, as compared to close-quarter fighting, he would have opted for a weapon like the M-16.

Even now, with the helicopter some forty yards off, had Gadgets been afforded the luxury of a caddie standing behind him with a golfing bag full of different assault rifles, he might have chosen something different. "A little far for the Uzi, ain't it, Mr. Schwarz?" "You're right, Tommy. Give me the 5.56 for this hole...."

None of which was to say that Gadgets was seriously undergunned with the Uzi.

He began firing on full-auto, burning through the first 32-round clip in a matter of seconds, yanking it free and clapping in another to begin shorter bursts.

Off to their right, separated by several yards now, was Lyons.

Firing the Atchisson.

The Ironman crouched and clamped the weapon against his side, gripping it in his viselike hands as he loosed four 3-round full-auto bursts.

He figured that if Able Team got into action first, it would give them about a three-second gap before the return fire would be definitely lethal.

Four seconds max.

That meant three blasts from the Atchisson. And, because he was the Ironman and by nature always pushed things to the limit, go for one more as well.

There's a sort of "delayed-reaction pause" that Lyons, like most combat men, knew to exist when two groups of enemy soldiers suddenly confronted one another. It doesn't happen all the time, but it happens frequently enough to be worth considering.

Lyons was counting on that now.

For some strange reason, the side that gets into action first can often count on having a two- to four-second pause before the fire is returned. This is so, even if, had there been no fire, the other side could have gotten into action in a second or so.

Lyons and Blancanales and Gadgets had discussed the phenomenon in the past.

If Side A and Side B suddenly confronted each other, reaction time might mean that for either one it would take one to two seconds to get into action. The brain had to go through a target-recognition/shoot-or-take-cover decision before the man swung into action. It was lightening-fast, of course, but it still meant a delay of one or two seconds.

However, it did not follow from this that *both* sides would get into action in one to two seconds.

Instead, they knew that if Side A fired first, say in 1.1 seconds, Side B's reaction to the original surprise would be extended by the additional "surprise," so to speak, of the muzzle flame and sound and the knowledge that they were being fired upon.

This meant another delay for the shoot-or-take-cover decision, and another corresponding delay. In addition, the return fire would often be less accurate, hampered by the survival instinct awareness of being a target to ongoing gunfire. And, if one's companions were taking hits, and the peripheral vision and the hearing were realizing that men to the left and to the right were being maimed, the effect was magnified.

Gruesome shit, but true.

Lyons knew that when you worked in a gruesome business, you'd better not be too sensitive to this shit. Or more accurately, you'd better not let your sensitivities immobilize you or make you less effective.

Otherwise you wouldn't be in that business for very long.

But Lyons and the others knew something else as well. Despite how simple it looked to annihilate large numbers of men if they were coming at you in a group and you had automatic firepower available, in real life it wasn't that easy.

In other words, they were well aware that one could rake the ranks of the enemy with the autoburn. And, while heavy casualties—extremely heavy casualties—

would be inflicted, it was never one hundred percent. Or even ninety, or eighty, or seventy.

In the real world, fifty percent was damn good. And then the reaction-time delay would be used up.

As Lyons had once explained to some geek congressman or another, "If twenty of the assholes are coming at you, and you nail ten—in absolute terms, ten sounds like a helluva lot. But that still means there are ten men left to nail your ass when they get over the reaction time."

And there was always the chance that this particular enemy would be that unusual one, that one in ten or whatever the ratio was, who didn't experience the delayed reaction.

If so, Able Team would soon be the late Able Team. It all added to the pucker factor.

The Atchisson bucked in his grip as the Ironman clamped the trigger four successive times.

Each 3-shot burst sounded almost like a single blast, a long explosion that had a little stutter to it. The Atchisson's box magazine had been loaded with Lyons's favorite mixture of Magnum rounds, one double-ought buckshot, the next a slug, the next double-ought buckshot.

One time when he had been bored, Gadgets had gotten down the firearms tables and had calculated the approximate energy of each such burst.

The tables told him that each double-ought pellet from a 12-gauge Magnum round had at twenty yards between 140 and 155 foot-pounds of energy. Assuming that each round had twelve pellets, and using the conservative 140-foot-pound figure, that meant twelve times 140 or 1680 foot-pounds if the target absorbed the entire load.

The slug would have approximately 1800 foot-pounds at twenty yards, and when Gadgets added two rounds of buck plus the slug, the total came to a staggering 5160 foot-pounds of energy in the 3-round burst.

By comparison, Gadgets reported that a fairly hot load in a .357 Magnum or .45 pistol round would have in the range of 350 to 500 foot-pounds. The average .38 Special round would be lucky to have 275.

Now the Atchisson jerked in Lyons's hands as he fired the four blasts. He saw the orange muzzle flames begin to wink from the ranks of the soldiers as he fired the fourth blast, and knew it was high time to be moving.

The flames that looked long and streaklike didn't bother Lyons—personally—as much as the ones that looked like round dots. The round dots meant he was looking straight at them; the elongated ones were obviously fired at an angle and therefore not at him.

There seemed to be a hell of a lot of the round kind, he thought. Shit! This wasn't fair. How come they were shooting more at him than at the other two?

Of course, the Atchisson put out such a vivid orange fireball with each blast, he was the obvious target.

The Ironman sprinted for the front of the train. Fifteen feet later, he realized he wouldn't make it around the engines in time, so he made a shallow dive under the passenger car.

He tucked and rolled on his side, over the near rail and onto the bed of ties. Slugs clanked against the heavy steel rail and against the wheels of the car, making sparks as the lead spattered or the projectiles ricocheted into the distance. Lyons kept rolling up and over the other rail, then down the slight embankment on the other side.

Then he got to his feet and ran forward, intending to get around the front of the engine and lay down some fire at the advancing enemy.

Toward the rear of the train, Blancanales and Gadgets had been counting the seconds as they raked the shadowy forms with their assault rifles.

"Shit!"

Gadgets spit the oath as a trail of autoburn from one of the enemy zipped by his feet, peppering his lower legs with stone chips and bullet fragments. He felt one very solid chunk hit his calf, knocking that leg backward and causing him to end up momentarily on all fours. Then he, too, rolled sideways under the train.

The attackers had apparently been taken by surprise.

Had Lyons or Gadgets or the Politician had time to think about it, that fact would have indicated that Able Team's presence on the train had been unknown to the mole in the government. And their true purpose had apparently gone undetected by the train personnel as well.

Surprised or not, however, the attackers showed themselves to be both well-trained and fearless.

Ghost Train

There had in fact been a delay, but it was due to trained reactions rather than to indecision. Despite the surprise and the heavy losses from the deadly firepower Able Team had mustered, the attackers had reacted quickly, diving in all directions, rolling and then coming up in impromptu three-man fire teams.

The teams spread out and advanced, the commandos covering one another in their forward movement.

Blancanales read the attack instantly.

He had had the watch when the choppers came in. As a result, he was more prepared than his two colleagues.

As a skilled combat soldier, Blancanales had known they would probably have two or three seconds of delay after they began firing, just as Lyons and Gadgets had known it. As a friend of Carl Lyons, Blancanales also knew that the Ironman would probably push it to the max, and then some, quite possibly stretching the delay to, or past, the breaking point.

At about three seconds, therefore, the Politician stopped the M-16 fire. He reached quickly into a pouch around his waist and came out with another kind of antipersonnel weapon.

High-explosive fragmentation grenades.

He didn't want the enemy to be able to spread out. And, trained as he was, he saw instantly that that was exactly what was happening. Accordingly, rather than put the grenades into the center of the group of commandos, he planned to toss one right and one left, trying to "lead" them just enough so the soldiers at either end of the formation would take the blasts.

Keep clipping the wings, buddy, he thought, and save the body for later.

He tossed the first grenade at a spot he estimated to be five yards to the outside of the group of soldiers. He was right on target, and two of the hastily formed fire teams took the impact of the blast.

The other side was closer to the front of the train, and was a longer throw.

He wasn't quite so accurate with that one, and the grenade landed in the midst of the men rather than beyond the farthest fire team.

"Shit!" was Blancanales's only comment on the accuracy of his toss. Then he, too, was diving and rolling and scrambling under the train.

"No shit!" was Gadgets's shouted rejoinder.

When the second grenade went off, it wiped out several commandos, but some five or six men were already beyond it. Oh, well, thought the Politician, let Lyons worry about that.

As he and Gadgets rolled out the other side of the train, Blancanales suddenly became aware that the roar of engines was louder.

"What the—" he began.

Nearby, barely visible, Gadgets pointed upward. "There, Homes. We got company."

Straining his eyes through the fog, Blancanales made out the immense shape, darker than the rest of the misty darkness, of a second chopper descending on their side of the train.

19

The huge chopper made its way downward.

Unlike the helicopter on the other side of the train, this one had to be more careful in its maneuvering because the space was tight—at one point an electric line ran across the area.

Blancanales made some quick calculations.

Maybe, just maybe, it would give him enough time.

"I'm going inside!" he snapped to Gadgets.

"What for?"

"To have a beer. What else?"

Then the Politician was gone, pulling himself back inside the train.

Gadgets shrugged, then ran toward the end of the train, intending to lay down some fire at the enemy on the other side. A part of his mind wondered if any of the gunfire could damage the nuclear storage containers, and if so, what the result would be.

Maybe he'd be like some TV or movie monster, and become superhuman. Maybe grow nineteen-inch arms or develop the strength to lift three times as much as he was now capable of lifting.

Inside the train, Blancanales made his way back to his Pullman in haste.

He dashed inside the small compartment and dragged out a couple of pieces of luggage.

He selected a piece that was about four feet long, two feet wide and a foot high. Apart from its ungainly size, it resembled any other functional case, and it looked as if it might contain laboratory instruments or possibly a musical instrument.

On the outside were stenciled the words, Telescope. Fragile. Handle with care.

He opened the case and removed two of the three-foot-long tubes that were the LAW rockets they had packed with such care back at Stony Man Farm.

The Politician pivoted and started to rise, the two tubes in his hands.

And found himself face to face with Beverly.

"Out of my way, Bev—" he started to say. Then his gaze fell on the Uzi carbine she was pointing at him.

For a moment it didn't register. This beautiful woman with the beautiful body was pointing an Uzi at him. It did not compute.

Then he looked again.

Gone was the friendly, dazzling smile. Gone was the flirtatious air of a woman who left the top button of her blouse strategically unbuttoned to give a hint of the voluptuous womanhood below. In its place was the fiery determination of the fanatic, a woman who would kill and die for her cause.

She had been a plant all along, he realized.

Moreover, in that instant, he mentally kicked himself for not seeing the signs, though in fairness to himself they had not been that obvious. She had said she was "the new girl," he recalled, a last-minute substitute for somebody else. And, in some vague, indefinable way, she had never seemed quite genuine.

He wouldn't get to use the LAW on the descending chopper. It meant that more soldiers would be let off, and Able Team and its mission would be history. Ashes to ashes, dust to dust.

Oh, well, Blancanales thought, if that's what happens, that's what happens. To put it the way Lyons did, it was fun while it lasted.

Looking at his Uzi death warrant in the hands of that fanatic woman, the Politician smiled his best smile.

"So, Beverly, do you know how to use that?"

"I am not Beverly. I am Kara," she announced.

"Who?"

"Kara. Commander of the New World Insurrectionists. And I am going to kill you."

Outside, the roar of the descending chopper grew louder.

Blancanales wondered why she didn't just do it. Hell, that was what he would have done. Either she wanted him to know who she was, or she wanted him alive to be tortured, or maybe symbolically executed.

She answered his unspoken question.

"You and your friends surprised us," she said. "But we are superior in training and numbers. The others will be killed, but we want one of you for interrogation and execution as a symbol against the oppression of your government."

The Politician grinned even more broadly. He was taking a hell of a gamble, he knew. Still, she had said she wanted him alive, and in his experience fanatics tended to follow through on things like that.

Besides, when the chances are slim and none, slim looks pretty damn good.

"If the interrogation includes torture, would you mind getting one of the others?" he said with a wink. "I hate being tortured. It sucks. In fact—"

Kara gestured with the Uzi. "You will not make jokes!" she snapped, the color rising in her cheeks. "The others are dead, and you soon will be."

"Others?"

"The engineers and the scientists, the dumpy old man and the pretty-boy co-worker. Now place your hands behind your head. Now!"

Blancanales saw the gleam in her eyes when she referred to the others, now deceased. It was a gleam that went beyond fanaticism, into the realm of the twisted. To put it bluntly, he decided, she was completely, one hundred percent insane.

Outside the train the helicopter was now only fifteen feet off the ground.

Moving slowly, he set down the two long tubes. He put his arms over his head and laced his fingers together, then lowered his hands behind his neck in the classic pose of the captured prisoner. As he did this, he spoke.

"The civilians are dead? You killed them?"

As he had hoped, talking about her favorite subject proved to be a distraction.

"Yes. I killed them. It was easy, and I enjoyed it, I enjoyed watching them die, those fascists, those oppressors, those...*men*."

Slowly, the Politician's two thumbs extended downward behind his neck. Slowly, they gripped the metallic object in the center of his back. And equally slowly, they eased it upward until he didn't have to use the two thumbs to grip it, but could hold it by the thumb and forefinger of his right hand.

"Men?" he repeated, making a smile and a wink as he spoke. "What have you got against men...?"

Then his hand flashed forward and he was throwing himself to one side, in case the gun went off anyway.

The razor-sharp throwing dagger buried itself into Kara's throat, just above the top center of her rib cage. It went in clear up to the hilt, so that the sharp point just broke the skin on the back.

She made a single, gagging cough, and staggered backward. Her eyes went wide with shock. Blancanales stepped quickly forward and knocked the sagging Uzi from her grasp with his own bare hands. Then he drew his .45 Colt Government Model from his belt and shot her once between the eyes.

He didn't wait to see her fall.

Turning back, Blancanales grabbed one of the LAW tubes. The chopper was almost on the ground now, maybe thirty yards out, steadying to descend farther.

The Politician stood back and kicked the glass window out with the heavy sole of his boot. Then, he extended the tube and, without bothering to try to find the dark shape in the sighting apparatus, he eyeballed his target and let fly.

Fully extended, the LAW's tube was some four and a half feet long. With a click and a whoosh, the short-burning rocket ignited in the tube and fired.

An instant later, the chopper exploded into a petrochemical ball of orange flame that roiled up into the night sky.

Grabbing the other LAW, Blancanales ran out of the train and rejoined Gadgets. When he got there he saw that, on the other side of the train, it was all over but the mop-up—except for a third chopper that was starting to pull up, as if it had changed its mind.

Again by eyeball, the Politician launched the second LAW at that helicopter. And all but missed.

The rocket hit high, clipping off the main rotor. The explosion failed to ignite the chopper's fuel, however, so the mechanical monster did not burst into a fireball as the other one had.

Instead, it made an abrupt sideways swoop, and crashed about fifteen yards from Lyons's end of the train, where the Ironman still crouched, blasting at the enemy with the Atchisson.

Blancanales waited for the fireball.

For some odd reason, the chopper did not explode immediately on impact. Most of its occupants were killed in the crash, however, or died in the fire that broke out some six or eight seconds later. The explosion followed a couple of seconds after that.

But one man had staggered from the machine before it exploded.

Dazed, he wandered away from the chopper, conscious only of the need to get clear of the wreckage, of the death and destruction.

Then he became conscious of something else.

This was America, country of laws and courts and legal loopholes and technicalities. America, where lawyers fought the final battles with words and case citations, not bullets.

America, where the police treated you civilly if you got arrested. They had to. The courts would be unhappy with them if they didn't.

The daze clearing, Vince Danelli raised his hands above his head.

"Don't shoot!" he shouted. "I surrender. Don't shoot. I'm coming peacefully."

From the front of the train, an ear-splitting blast erupted as the Atchisson fired yet again, three rounds, two of double-ought buck and the middle one a single slug.

The range was perhaps twenty feet.

Buckshot doesn't spread much at that short a distance.

All but a couple of the pellets found their target.

Five thousand, one hundred sixty foot-pounds of energy—give or take a few hundred—struck their target.

Carl Lyons had no way of knowing it at the time, but he had just avenged the murder of his woman.

EPILOGUE

"Coke," said Brognola.

"Huh?"

"Coke, Ironman. You know. Cocaine. Cola. Snow. White magic. That stuff idiots and weaklings put up their noses to make them feel good."

"I know what it is, Chief. What about it?"

They were at Stony Man Farm. Not in the conference room, but in Brognola's office. Gadgets and Blancanales were there also, the former in a chair to keep the weight off his injured leg.

"That's what this caper was all about," said Brognola at last.

"Coke?"

"Yeah, coke."

"I thought we were guarding the ingredients for your basic thermonuclear warhead, Chief. Where does coke come into it?"

Brognola chomped on a cigar. "You were also guarding, it turns out, the biggest shipment of cocaine ever snared by the narcs. Possibly the biggest single shipment ever made in this country, though the stats are incomplete as to that."

"Where?"

"On that train." The chief leaned forward. "Look. Do you remember two cars with separate containers on them? One wasn't supposed to be there."

Lyons recalled the incident in which Gadgets had accidentally made reference to the manifest or cargo schedule of the train, and the anonymous container that they had joked was okay as long as it didn't have a bomb in it.

"Yes, Chief," he said at last.

"Well, it turns out that container had six tons of almost pure cocaine in it."

Lyons thought that over. Finally, he asked, "Did you know about that when you sent us in, Chief?"

"Negative. We didn't know about it until the mop-up after your little fun and games in the train yard."

"Oh."

"Carl, my boy," said Brognola, his voice soft, "there are times, a lot of times, when I send you in blindfolded. I hate it every time I do it. But this wasn't one of them."

Lyons nodded. "Not with respect to the coke, anyway," he said at last.

Brognola stared at him. "What do you mean by that?"

Lyons's response was oblique. "Did you plug the leak?"

For several long moments, the chief looked at him. Then, finally, his face split into the merry grin they knew so well. "Carl, my lad," he boomed, "you never cease to amaze me. Of course, I should have known it."

"Known what, Chief?"

"That you guys would figure it out. After all, you are the best. And yes, there was a leak. And yes, we found it and plugged it. While we're on the subject, would you care to know what this caper was really all about?"

"Sure, Chief. If it's not too much trouble, that is."

"No trouble. What it was about was coke. And the Mafia."

"The Mafia?" echoed Lyons. "What the hell does the Mafia want with nuclear bombs?"

Brognola explained what the investigation had revealed in the aftermath of the caper.

The Mafia, it seemed, couldn't care less about the nuclear materials. But they did have an interest, a vital interest, in the six tons of cocaine.

It turned out the mob had a mole, an informer, in the government, the Nuclear Regulatory Commission, to be exact. Ironically, they had developed the leak through a union corruption caper they had done, involving a power plant. But, because nukes are nukes, at least in the eyes of some bureaucrats, the leak knew about the ghost train even though its contents were military, not power-plant stuff.

When the mob found out about the secret ghost trains, they decided it would be an ideal way to move a massive quantity of coke from San Diego—where it had entered the country—to Chicago, where it was needed.

"In a way, the plan was brilliant," acknowledged Brognola. "And gutsy."

"Seems risky as hell to me," observed Gadgets.

"Yes and no. The hard part was getting it onto the train. But once it was there, it was safe as could be. After all, the ghost train moved in complete secrecy. Once the mob had fooled two or three key people to get the coke on board, nobody, but nobody, was going to mess with it."

Lyons nodded. "That is pretty slick, I guess," he said at last.

Brognola nodded. "The train's strongest point—its secrecy—proved to be its weakest, in that regard."

They thought that over. Finally, Blancanales spoke up. "So how did the New World Insurrectionists fit in?"

"Simple. They were muscle, and they were a diversion. The Mafia used them, and they used the Mafia."

"How so, Chief?"

"The NWI would hijack the train. They, not the mob, did that part of the dirty work. They wanted the nuke stuff for themselves, and the mob couldn't have cared less about that. But after it was over, the manhunt would center on the NWI, not the Mafia. Since the coke was never on the train—officially—nobody would miss it, and nobody would look to the mob."

Lyons whistled. He had to admit, it wasn't just slick, it was brilliant.

Brognola nodded. "It was the ultimate symbiotic relationship," he said.

Blancanales wrinkled his brow. "Say what? The what kind of relationship?

Gadgets answered. "Symbiotic. It comes from symbiosis. It means, 'You scratch my back, and I'll scratch yours.' Two separate entities with nothing in common, each benefit from doing something that helps the other."

"*Gracias, amigo.*" The Politician's voice had just a tinge of sarcasm to it, which he offset by his broad, Blancanales smile.

"The Mafia, it seems, was there in one of the choppers to airlift away the cargo container that had the coke. And if we—that is, you guys—hadn't been there, it would have worked."

"And Beverly, aka Kara?" asked Gadgets. "She was a NWI commando?"

"Yes. She killed the other technician, and substituted herself, to be an insider on the train. Apparently you guys did a good job of concealing your purpose there. She was suspicious, but that's all."

It was Lyons who spoke next. When he did, his voice was low and sad.

"And Julie?" he asked.

Brognola's face softened. "Killed because she was bringing the Lambda file to you. The Mafia informer knew about that, and told his contact in the mob. They killed her to try to find out what the FBI knew about their plans. And, incidentally, to see if the file identified an informant they suspected was in their organization."

"Who ordered it?" asked the Ironman flatly.

"Two men, apparently."

"Who?"

"One of them was an L.A. and San Diego mobster named Vince Danelli. He's already been taken care of."

"How?"

"Seems he was on the scene as a supervisor, so to speak. Somebody, and I won't say who, caught him at about twenty feet with about twenty-three pellets of double-ought buck and a rifled slug. Shot the shit out of him, to be precise."

Lyons didn't respond. So that was the guy who came out of the downed chopper, he thought.

"The other man," said Brognola, "is a Chicago mob kingpin named Powers."

"Powers!" exclaimed Lyons.

Brognola nodded. "Yep. Apparently that was what Julie was trying to tell our friend Gadgets here. Though how she happened to know that is a mystery."

Lyons seemed lost in his own private thoughts. "She was a good investigator," he said distractedly, "even if she was a woman."

Brognola said softly. "I'm sorry, Carl."

"Yeah." The Ironman still sounded distracted. Then he focussed again, and looked at Brognola.

"Powers," he said.

"What about him?"

"I want him."

"I sort of figured you would."

"Can I have him?"

Brognola relit his cigar, which had gone out again. Then he spoke through the smoke.

"You can have him."

From the Chicago *Daily Sun*, July 15, 1987, Evening Edition:

Mafia Boss Dies in Fall

Reputed Chicago Mafia figure Axis Powers died late yesterday afternoon when he plunged 42 stories from his office. Police are investigating the death.

Details are sketchy, but according to one police spokesman Powers, 56, fell out of the window of his office on the forty-second floor of the First National Bank Building.

The police spokesman said that the windows of the First National Bank Building do not open. Also, they are constructed from a special reinforced safety glass, so it would be virtually impossible to break one accidentally. The investigation is proceeding on the theory that Powers may have been the victim of a gangland slaying.

The deceased was a long-time Chicago resident. He was on the board of trustees of the symphony orchestra, a generous donor to the American Civil Liberties Union, and was active in several other other civic organizations.

AVAILABLE NOW!

JAMES AXLER
DEATHLANDS
Crater Lake

The struggle for survival continues.... Beneath the depths of the calm blue waters of Crater Lake, Ryan Cawdor and his intrepid companions discover the existence of a world more terrifying than their own. A huge cavern houses a community of crazed scientists—madmen who have developed new methods of mass destruction. They are now ready to test their weapons....

Crater Lake—the fourth book continuing the adventure and suspense of the bestselling DEATHLANDS saga.

Available now at your favorite retail outlet or reserve your copy for shipping by sending your name, address, zip or postal code along with a check or money order for $3.70 (includes 75 cents for postage and handling) payable to Gold Eagle Books to:

<u>In the U.S.</u>
Gold Eagle Books
901 Fuhrmann Blvd.
Box 1325
Buffalo, NY 14269-1325

<u>In Canada</u>
Gold Eagle Books
P.O. Box 609
Fort Erie, Ontario
L2A 5X3

Please specify book title with your order.

DL-4R

Available soon!

DON PENDLETON's
MACK BOLAN
TROPIC HEAT

The probing tentacles of the drug network have crept far enough into the streets of America. The only solution is to cut the cancer out at the source. The only man equal to the task is Mack Bolan!

SB-9

Available in SEPTEMBER at your favorite retail outlet or reserve your copy for August shipping by sending your name, address, zip or postal code, along with a check or money order for $4.70 (includes 75¢ postage and handling) payable to Gold Eagle Books to:

In the U.S.	In Canada
Gold Eagle Books	Gold Eagle Books
P.O. Box 1325	P.O. Box 609
901 Fuhrmann Blvd.	Fort Erie, Ontario
Buffalo, NY 14269-1325	L2A 5X3

Please specify book title with your order.

GOLD EAGLE

TAKE 'EM NOW

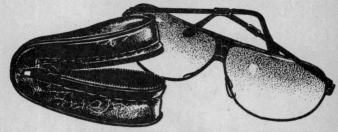

FOLDING SUNGLASSES FROM GOLD EAGLE

Mean up your act with these tough, street-smart shades. Practical, too, because they fold 3 times into a handy, zip-up polyurethane pouch that fits neatly into your pocket. Rugged metal frame. Scratch-resistant acrylic lenses. Best of all, they can be yours for only $6.99.

MAIL YOUR ORDER TODAY.

Send your name, address, and zip code, along with a check or money order for just $6.99 + .75¢ for postage and handling (for a total of $7.74) payable to Gold Eagle Reader Service. (New York and Iowa residents please add applicable sales tax.)

Remove from pouch...

unfold once...

Gold Eagle Reader Service
901 Fuhrmann Blvd.
P.O. Box 1396
Buffalo, N.Y. 14240-1396

unfold twice...

and they're ready to wear.

Offer not available in Canada.